EDELWEISS PIRATES:

Operation Einstein

M. A. Cooper

ISBN-13: 978-1530804641
ISBN-10: 1530804647

To the German people who resisted,

this book is dedicated to you.

Table of Contents

Prologue..1

Chapter One 3

Chapter Two 11

Chapter Three 17

Chapter Four 21

Chapter Five...33

Chapter Six 41

Chapter Seven..47

Chapter Eight...55

Chapter Nine..59

Chapter Ten 75

Chapter Eleven...79

Chapter Twelve..87

Chapter Thirteen 95

Chapter Fourteen 103

Chapter Fifteen 107

Chapter Sixteen...115

Chapter Seventeen 123

Chapter Eighteen 131

Chapter Nineteen 135

Chapter Twenty 141

Chapter Twenty-One 151

Chapter Twenty-Two..157

Chapter Twenty-Three..163

Chapter Twenty-Four..169

Chapter Twenty-Five..185

Chapter Twenty-Six..193

Chapter Twenty-Seven 197

Chapter Twenty-Eight 207

Chapter Twenty-Nine 213

Chapter Thirty..231

Chapter Thirty-One..235

Chapter Thirty-Two 243

Prologue

Nazi Germany, also known as the Third Reich, launched its invasion of Poland in 1939 followed by invading France and Norway in 1940. The persecution and atrocities carried out by the Nazi regime against the Jewish population and the euthanasia of people with mental or physical disabilities are notorious and well documented.

The oppression and strict regime also affected the lives of normal patriotic German people. Teenagers rebelled over the forced closer of dance clubs, Jazz halls, and new rules outlawing youth groups such as the Boy Scouts.

It became compulsory for all teenagers to join the Hitler Youth. Some teens did enjoy the discipline and Hitler Youth activities while some of the rebellious teens formed their own secret groups, the most famous and largest group of all was known as the Edelweiss Pirates. In 1944 at the peak of WW2 there was estimated to be over 100,000 Edelweiss Pirates across Germany or German occupied Europe.

Chapter One

All eyes darted across the classroom towards Austin; a few giggles even caught the attention of history teacher Miss Stephens. She looked over her glasses and dared anyone to make a sound. Austin was squirming in his seat. The narrator mentioned the name 'Schmidt' a second time.

Black and white images appeared on the screen showing emaciated corpses thrown in a mass grave. It was nauseating to watch, as some were clearly children. The teenage viewers in Miss Stephens's history class had mixed emotions ranging from disgust to sorrow. Light relief came when their classmate's surname was the same as a ruthless Nazi officer cited in the documentary.

Fourteen-year-old Austin Schmidt's iPhone vibrated silently in his pocket. After a careful check to see where Miss Stephens's gaze was, he slipped it out and looked down at the screen. It was a text message from his mother,

Don't be late home after school, Dad said our flight is leaving an hour early; we will get a pizza

3

for you and Sam to eat at Nana & Grandpas'. luv
Mom XXX

Austin chewed his bottom lip in annoyance, mainly because of the way she spelt 'Luv.' She was trying to act 'cool' as she would call it. He was looking forward to spending the weekend at his grandparents' home, although he would enjoy it more if Samantha, his nine-year-old sister wasn't going to be there. Last time they stayed for the weekend his grandfather was going to let him shoot his gun in the back yard, but his grandmother had rejected the idea because Samantha wanted to do it as well and Gran said she was too young. It meant none of them could shoot it. And then there was the time when his grandfather was going to let him have a small glass of wine with dinner, but again Samantha wanted some too, so none of them had any.

He knew it was wrong to have bad thoughts about her, like wishing he was an only child or wishing she was a boy. Instead he had the world's most annoying little sister, who always went into his room, even if he was getting dressed, always went on his computer, hung around when he had *HIS* friends over and if he tried to push her out of his room she would scream so much you would think the house was on fire. She was a brilliant actress who could cry at will and blame Austin for causing her pain or being nasty to her, even if he had done nothing.

Austin was not well known at school; he was almost invisible to most with just above average grades. He was teased for being a redhead, in the summer his face would amass freckles that he hated. His best friend, Colin Pearson, was often teased for being a nerd, but they supported each other and when they stuck together they didn't get bullied too often.

They had been friends since first grade. They went through middle school together and now were attending their freshman year at Stroundsburg High. The Pennsylvanian high school would prepare them for college.

"Homework will be a five-hundred-word essay on what you think it would be like to be a freshman during WWII in Germany. Imagine yourselves as German teenagers and what life was like during the war," Miss Stephens barked. A few anonymous groans went around the room; they knew they had history again on Monday so it meant it had to be done over the weekend along with math homework. "Use the Internet for research but the work must be original. Think about what you would be doing -- clubs, after school activities -- and remember as teenagers. Your fathers would probably have been away at war."

"Austin Schmidt would be shooting Jews," Scott McCamant grinned. A roar of laughter went around the class. Austin eyed him and said nothing.

"We will have none of that; it's not a laughing matter. Just because one Nazi officer in the documentary was called Schmidt does not mean it was Austin's relation. I suspect Schmidt is quite a common name in Germany. Besides, most of the Nazis were hunted down and dealt with after the war for 'war crimes,'" Miss Stephens chastised. "Austin, I've met your German grandfather. Was he in the war?"

Austin's normally pale white face turned as red as his spiky hair; he chewed his lip again. "Um, no he was too young," Austin softly replied. He loathed being the center of attention.

"Do you know when he was born?"

"Um. He was born, um. He's eighty four so he was born in 1928." Miss Stephen's eyes gazed at the ceiling for a second while she thought.

"Then he would have been your age during the war. He could help you with your homework." She smiled. "It will be interesting to get a real account." She paused again. "He would have most certainly been in the Hitler Youth; it was compulsory for boys fourteen to sixteen."

"Miss, in the documentary it said that some of the Hitler Youth carried out punishment on the Jews. So I was right," Scott joked. Austin gave

Scott an angry glare that was picked up by Miss Stephens. She quickly tried to defuse the attack on Austin's grandfather.

"Scott, that will be enough of that. Every German boy and many in German occupied countries had to join the Hitler youth; you always get a few bad eggs. Can anyone tell me what very famous person was also a Hitler Youth member?"

Blank faces stared back at her. Scott eventually held up his hand.

"Yes Scott?" She asked.

"Was Austin's grandfather famous?" His remark was welcomed by more laughter from his classmates but a stern look from Miss Stephens.

"Scott, sometimes I wonder if you'll ever grow up. No. It is, in fact, His Holiness, the Pope'. Pope Benedict XVI. He was born in Germany and as a fourteen-year-old also joined the Hitler Youth."

The bell rang, and the normal scramble for the door and hum of chatter and chairs scraping across the floor started. Austin sighed at his friend Colin as he followed him out toward lunch.

They sat together in the canteen. Austin slurped on his chocolate milk while Colin stuffed French fries into his mouth with one hand while scrolling a menu on his iPhone with his other hand. "I could do with your grandfather's help with my history paper. I fell asleep and missed most of that documentary."

Colin garbled with a full mouth. Austin smiled back at him.

"I'm staying at his house this weekend so I can email you some stuff, but *don't* copy it word for word like last time I helped you," Austin grinned.

Heads turned in the canteen because of the commotion that started in the main doorway; a chanting and shouting began as if someone was shouting orders. It soon became apparent what was going on. Scott McCamant and three other boys marched into the canteen. They held their left hands up to their faces with two fingers parallel held under noses to simulate a 'Hitler Moustache' similar to what they had just seen in the history documentary. They marched in with right arms saluting up and legs being kicked waist high.

"Achtung. Achtung. Austin Schmidt, ve need you to kill some Jews. Can ve count on you?" Scott barked, trying to sound German.

Austin was out of his seat before Colin could hold him back. He took a swing at Scott and caught him square on his nose. Scott's legs gave in and he crumpled on the floor. A river of blood started to gush from his nose.

A hush engulfed the canteen. Immediately Austin felt remorse for his actions. He had never hit anyone before and was surprised as much as everyone else that he had knocked Scott off his feet with one punch.

He offered a hand to help Scott up but it was brushed away.

Chapter Two

Mrs. Schmidt was called into school to collect Austin since he was facing a possible suspension for the assault on Scott. The only thing saving him for now was that Scott had been in trouble so many times before and what he had said about killing Jewish people would not be tolerated. Plus, up until now, Austin had a clean record. Since the principal was away at a governor's meeting, he would discuss it with both sets of parents on Monday. As soon as he climbed into his mother's car she chastised him.

"Of all the days for you to start fighting in school you choose today. You know how important this weekend is for your father; we have a million things to do before we catch the plane. The last thing I needed was this. Fighting. What has gotten into you?"

"Mom he--" Austin was interrupted before he could answer her question.

"Save it for your father; I don't want to hear it," she screamed, banging the palm of her hand on the steering wheel.

Austin gazed out the window and rolled his eyes; he was trying to think of his punishments.

Grounded for sure, one, maybe two, weeks, extra chores no doubt, no computer? No he needed that for homework. Austin decided that his father would ground him and give him extra chores.

For the rest of the journey home his mother never spoke to him, She tutted occasionally, huffed and puffed, shook her head a few times, and drove erratically. Austin thought he got off quite well with his mom; now it was just his dad he had to answer to.

*

The Schmidt family hurried to their grandparents' home; Austin's parents would have to drop him and Samantha off then and head straight to the airport. Samantha sat back in the car selecting songs on her iPod; she had just one earplug in her left ear; the other dangled above her waist. She wanted to hear all the gory details as her father ripped into Austin. She twirled her red hair around her finger, enjoying the moment while her big brother was severely reprimanded. She grinned when she heard her father mention that Austin was also to empty the dishwasher every morning. That was normally her chore.

Austin said nothing. When he was asked what he had to say for himself he was cut off again in mid-sentence as he tried to explain. The journey couldn't end soon enough for Austin. The family arrived at his grandparents' home and Austin never even said goodbye to his parents. He just took his school bag and clothing bag up to the bedroom he used and watched out the window as his parents said goodbye to his grandparents and Sam. His grandfather looked up at his bedroom window and caught Austin's eye. Austin felt guilty for not saying goodbye; he flopped onto the bed and gazed at the ceiling.

A knock came at the door. "Austin." His grandfather called to him. Austin jumped off the bed and opened the door. "Your grandmother has warmed up the pizza, I have some root beer open for you, come down and join us."

"I'm not really hungry Grandpa," Austin lied.

"I heard you had some trouble today. Come down and eat with us and tell me what happened."

Austin followed his grandfather down the stairs and slumped down next to his sister at the table. He was just about to put some pizza in his mouth when Sam started to gloat.

"Gran I will have to start a new hobby now that I have *so* much free time on my hands."

"Oh and why is that dear?" Gran asked. Sam explained that she no longer had to do her chores now that Austin was going to do them since he was grounded for four weeks. Austin dropped his pizza back on his plate, got up, and slumped back up stairs. He felt bad enough without her rubbing it in.

A knock at Austin's door came twenty minutes later. This time his grandfather slowly opened it and found Austin lying on his stomach on his bed.

"I'm not hungry," Austin snapped.

"Good, because the pizza is all gone." His grandfather smiled.

Austin turned and, with squinted eyes, glared at is grandfather. "I haven't eaten all day. I was at lunch when the fight happened. I'm starving really."

His grandfather sat on his bed and gently patted his back. "I know; that's why I put your pizza in the oven. Come on, let's go into my study and eat it. Your sister and grandmother are making cupcakes so we can talk, man to man."

Classified as an adult and being called a man appealed to Austin. He smiled at his grandfather and followed him back downstairs.

His grandfather's study always fascinated Austin. He had models of aircrafts hanging from the ceiling and vintage pistols hung on the walls, many over a hundred years old. His desk had a model of a German Zeppelin airship, next to that a brass nameplate bearing his name -- 'Frederick Schmidt. On the fair wall hung a mounted deer head. A shelf supported a taxidermy rabbit, fox, and squirrel—all looking like they were stalking each other. When Austin was younger he had always felt like their eyes where hunting him, watching his every move, waiting to pounce.

He was passed a plate full of pizza.

"So, Austin, what's this all about? I know boys fight from time to time and I can understand that your sister annoyed you. Your aunt had the same effect on your father when he was your age. But there's more to it; come on spit it out." His grandfather warmly smiled.

Chapter Three

"Grandpa, were you a Nazi?" Austin asked, biting into a slice of pizza. "Agh it's hot," he yelled, spitting it out again.

"I forgot to turn the oven on so I put it in the microwave," Grandpa chuckled before looking more serious. "No, son, I was never a Nazi."

"But were you in the Hitler Youth?" Austin asked, picking off a piece of pepperoni.

"No, far from it. I hated them." He smiled and took down an old photograph album from a top shelf. He lovingly stroked the front of it before gently opening the cover.

Grandpa flipped through the pictures showing Austin a picture of himself when he was Austin's age at around fourteen years old. Another picture showed his grandfather's parents, Austin's great grandparents. The next page disturbed and disappointed Austin. It was a picture of a German soldier with the same boy next to him. The next picture was a teenager in a Hitler Youth uniform.

"This is my father. He was a carpenter, like me, but was called up to serve his country. This picture was taken of him and me the day before he left; I never saw him again. He was killed."

Austin studied the pictures. "So he would have been my great grandfather?" Austin turned his attention to the Hitler Youth; below the photograph had some writing. "This says Frederick Schmidt age fourteen, but you just said you weren't in the Hitler Youth."

His grandfather exhaled deeply. "Well I suppose at one point, technically, I was, but it's a long story and the truth was the complete opposite."

"I have all weekend Grandpa, I'm doing history homework and I want to know everything. Did you help kill the Jews?"

His grandfather slammed the photo album shut; he was angered by his grandson's question.

"This is stuff I have not even told your father about, and your grandmother knows very little about it and what actually happened."

Austin gently took the photo album back and carried on looking at the pictures. "Please tell me, Grandpa."

His grandfather took a deep breath and spoke in a tone Austin had never heard before. "Austin, you can never look back. The past is a land best never revisited, for it houses a landscape that can never be changed. All the bad things that ever happened live there, frozen in time, waiting to haunt you ... waiting to wrap you in chains and drag you to the bottom of despair, knowing that you cannot change them but knowing that they can have a dire effect on you".

He sat back in his chair behind his desk, took off his spectacles and looked at Austin. "I have not been back to Germany since I left at the age of seventeen in 1945; if you're not totally absorbed with nostalgia and desire to visit the old country then why bother?" Austin pulled a chair up to the desk and watched his grandfather as he spoke. His thinning hair was white now but still showed a few tinges of red around his ears.

"I was fourteen, the same age as you are now. I guess it started around September or October 1942. I lived with my grandfather after my father was killed. Gunthrie Schmidt was his name, but all my friends and I called him Grandpa Gunthrie." He proudly smiled as he thought and spoke of his own grandfather and recalled the events of his past.

Chapter Four

Würzburg, Germany 1942

The police fired a warning shot that splintered into the trees.

"Halt!" one of them yelled.

"I should Cuckoo," the old man wheezed beneath a wicked grin. He tucked the dead rabbit under his arm and scampered down the bank through the trees, sliding on the damp fallen leaves.

Two more shots rang out. This time they were aiming at the poacher. A bullet ricocheted off a tree just missing his hand. He pulled out his pistol and fired a warning shot of his own, being careful to make sure it went out of harm's way and into the air.

The policemen were startled and dove to the ground; the last thing they expected was to be shot at. They had only taken the job with the police force because most of the force's original policemen had been made to join the German army to fight for the country. These guys, instead, were in there sixties and not prepared to get hurt.

The old poacher made it to the riverbank where his rowboat was waiting. He clambered into the small craft, almost toppling into the water and cast off. The strong current dragged the wooden boat along.

The two policemen finally got the courage to climb down the bank, only to see the boat moving off in the distance. Frustrated, they fired a final shot at him, but he was safely out of range.

The old man picked up the rabbit he had illegally hunted, held its front foot between his fingers, and made the rabbit wave goodbye to his pursuers. "Say bye bye, bunny," Gunthrie chuckled.

The two police scanned the area, exasperated he had gotten away yet again. They had a good idea who he was but could never catch him red-handed.

Gunthrie Schmidt had just turned sixty-three; he was a disheveled and cantankerous, yet lovable, old rogue, always getting into scrapes. He had studied his craft of hunting –everything from hare, rabbit, pheasant to deer, and trout since he was a boy. Even the odd sheep often made its way into Gunthrie's sack. He called himself a hunter living off the land. To others he was a poacher and recognized as a specialist dealing on the black market. He was no stranger to being chased by the Federal Ministry of Agriculture, local police, gamekeepers, and landowners.

The erratic German economy and strict food rationing was a boom to Gunthrie's business activities. He looked after his only grandson,

Frederick Schmidt, in a decrepit farmhouse, its cracked walls and shriveled beams constantly threatened by the destructive power of a boisterous red-haired fourteen-year-old boy.

Authorities had tried in vain to pin something on Gunthrie, but so far nothing had stuck. The German Pigeon Racing Association had banned him for life for cheating. He used two 'look-a-like' pigeons and got caught, and as he was on stage collecting his prize money and trophy, the second pigeon turned up and perched on his shoulder. Then there was the time he entered a fishing contest at Würzburg Main River. He won a trophy and prize money for the largest fish, until the judges realized his fish was a sea bass, a saltwater fish that could never have been caught in the freshwater river. He later admitted to friends in the pub, after he'd a few drinks, that he bought it at the market.

*

A group of five teenagers, all fourteen-year-olds, met up as usual after school. Most teens' fathers where either dead or away at war. By congregating together they could laugh, joke, and dream of becoming rich and famous someday; it was a release from the ongoing war. At fourteen they were too old to play with toys and too young to go and drink at bars. Boy Scouts and Girl Guides were banned. Fredrick and his friends wanted nothing to do with joining the Hitler Youth, so they sat around together and tried to make the most of the depressing times that living through a war brings.

"Edelweiss Pirates? Who are they? Sounds pretty lame to me. How hard can they be to be named after a flower." Frederick Schmidt laughed. "They might just as well call themselves the Pansy Pirates."

"No, they're tough; they fight the Hitler Youth," Helmut argued with a mouth full of apple strudel. He paused to wipe the crumbs off his sweater, stopping and plucking a larger piece of pastry between his chubby fingers that was stuck to his sweater, swiftly popping it in his already full mouth. "I heard my mother say they also deflated the tires of a Nazi general's car."

A contagious grin ran across the group's faces at the thought of doing something ghastly to the Nazis. For too long their lives had been diminished by the regime. They were no longer allowed to listen to Jazz music; young girls were forbidden from wearing make up. Some of their friends and families had disappeared, local Jewish owned businesses forced to close.

Eva Freck was the only girl in the group of five; she had an older brother Luis who was a loyal member of the Hitler Youth. Eva was somewhat of a tomboy, but these past few months she had grown up and started taking better care of her appearance.

The rest of the group was made up of four boys;
they were Helmut, Karl, Fritz, and Frederick. All
five of them started kindergarten together and were
very close.

Frederick Schmidt was a tough kid who'd
swing a fist at anyone who upset him. It was easy to
tell him apart from the others because he always
smelled of pig poo and his red hair was too long and
tangled. His mother died when he was seven, his
father when he was ten, so since then it'd been up to
his grandfather Gunthrie, to raise the boy. It was
only to be expected that Frederick would turn out
rough. Gunthrie wasn't exactly a good role model.
Frederick liked hanging out with his friends and
enjoyed going on hunting trips with his Grandpa.

"How do we join them?" Frederick gasped
excitedly.

"I thought you said they sounded pretty lame.
What did you call them, Pansy Pirates?" Eva teased.

Fritz stood and spat out the piece of straw he
was sucking. "Count me in. I've wanted to give it to
the Hitler Youth for months. They parade around
like they own the town. My aunt was at the grocery
store buying bread and they pushed her aside and
demanded to be served first. I could take most of
them in a fistfight; you just watch me I will. I hope
they get bombed by the Brits."

He looked at Eva and remembered her brother
Luis had joined them. "Sorry Eva, I used to like

Luis, but he is as despicable as the others. Luis was present when the Steinberg family was thrown out of the hotel they had owned for years, just because they were Jewish and so it could be offices for the Nazi party. Luis threw their clothing out a bedroom window onto the street along with the children's toys. Now that poor family's been forced to live with friends, their business and home stolen from them."

"He was following orders." Eva stood and faced Fritz; she paused and sat back down. "But, um…. he was laughing about it at the dinner table; I think the Nazis have brainwashed him."

"He never had any brains." Fritz argued. Karl finally stood; he held a presence that no one could describe. He was taller than Fritz, but then everyone was taller than Fritz. Karl would probably lose a fistfight, but he had a calming effect on people. Eva, like most girls, adored his good looks, but Eva also liked Fritz. Like most fourteen-year-old girls Eva discovered that she had feelings for boys. They no longer irritated her; she now laughed at their jokes and admired their looks. She was fond of both Karl and Fritz. They knew it and often tried to score points against each other.

"Fritz. Luis is her brother, so it's only right Eva defends him. Luis is only one Hitler Youth out of over a million members. Picking on her brother will just make *us* fight. We need to stick together and plan something to get back at them. It's now law that everyone between fourteen and eighteen join either the Hitler Youth or The League of German Girls. There's no way I'm going to wear the stupid uniform and be forced to do shameless things to the Jewish families. I will never do that; the Steinberg family was always nice to us. When I was a baby, and our home caught fire, the Steinbergs let my family stay at their hotel for little cost because we were neighbors. I agree we should join the Edelweiss Pirates and get back at the Hitler Youth."

Karl was the perfect German. He had blue eyes, blond hair that fell into his eyes, good looks and was very bright. He lived with his mother and blind older brother. Like Fredrick, he wore his hair long. Fritz was short for his age with short with dirty blond hair and blue/green eyes. Both his parents had died so he lived with his aunt in the town. He was the smallest of the group, Eva often called him cute, that being small made him look younger than his fourteen years.

Eva had blonde hair and large brown eyes; she often wore it in ponytails that danced on her shoulders. Being the only girl meant she was spoilt, especially by Fritz and Karl. The other member of the group was Helmut; the only way to describe him was that he was always eating and overweight.

The five of them started making suggestions; plans ranged from putting sugar in the gas tanks of

Nazi vehicles, rotten eggs thrown at passing cars, to actually fist fighting the Hitler Youth. One thing was abundantly clear; they would never do anything to harm the German army. That might've hurt Germany's effort to win the war. They all agreed they would never betray their country or 'Fatherland,' as they called it.

They came up with an idea to make weekend assaults on Hitler Youth leaders, to make their weekends a nightmare. They would start at the top this weekend with Colonel Manfred Von Furz. A fat highly decorated Nazi officer in his late sixties, he wore a large handlebar mustache. He was too old for regular military duty and was forced to retire from his original post to take a new position as the local leader of the Hitler Youth.

Most of the Hitler Youth boys hated him. He made them run laps across a cold and wet muddy field barefoot. At weekend camps they had to take cold showers; he told them it would toughen them up. He forced them to get into a makeshift ring to box each other. The smaller, more timid boys often went home from a Hitler Youth night with cuts and bruises on their faces.

The newly-formed Würzburg Edelweiss Pirates met at Frederick's farm. He took them to the barn, moved some bales of straw, and showed them a wooden trap door.

"This can be our secret bunker." Frederick puffed as he lifted the heavy wooden trap door up. He flicked a light switch inside the entrance. They all looked down into the gloomy room and followed him down.

"Got any food down there?" Helmut belched, going first and climbing down a wooden stepladder. Helmut was a food addict; he wasn't lazy or unfit, he just enjoyed food. Sausages and apple strudel were among his favorite foods, but anything that tasted good made him in foodie heaven. The result was a large waistband, round flushed red face with a small chin, and fat neck that gave him the appearance of a double chin. He lived with his mother who doted on him; her life revolved around Helmut. Since his father's death during the Polish invasion it got worse. She constantly was getting chastised by him for trying to comb his hair, straightening his clothing and fussing around him.

"Not unless you want to eat spiders," Eva replied. "This place is gross."

"It's a secret place. We can plan anything down here. It should even survive a bomb if the Tommie's start bombing us," Frederick argued.

"The Tommie's won't bomb out this far in the country. They're concentrating on the cities," Karl replied. "This place is perfect. Are you sure no one knows about it Frederick?"

"My grandpa Gunthrie does, but he said not to come down here since it was really filthy and stunk of cow piss."

"It *was* filthy and *did* stink of cow piss?" Eva scoffed, sarcastically waving her hand in front of her face as she climbed down and joined the others.

"You should have seen it three days ago. I spent the last three days cleaning it up."

"Yeah and you left all the trash from down there up in my workshop," A voice bellowed from the top of the wooden ladder. It was Frederick's grandfather, Grandpa Gunthrie. He slowly climbed down the steps carrying a bag full of Fanta sodas for the teens.

Grandpa Gunthrie was accepted by the teens; he was somewhat of a rebel himself. He sold food on the black market. Eggs, bacon, and fruit were rationed in Germany just like they were in most parts of the world during wartime. Grandpa Gunthrie knew farmers who wanted items that only he could get his hands on -- chocolate, fresh fruit, and even American made Nylon stockings. He could get his hands on most things. He was often in trouble for poaching or fishing where he shouldn't be.

To look at him you could easily mistake him for a hobo. He was round faced with white growth of facial hair. His pants were held up with twine; his waistcoat vest could not be done up because of his large stomach. Over everything he wore a dirty raincoat with patches on the elbows. Often his breath smelled of beer. But despite his shortcomings, the teens all thought he was fun to be around and allowed him to join in the meeting.

Grandpa Gunthrie suggested several things they could do to get revenge on the Nazis and the Hitler Youth. Anything he could suggest to attack the *establishment,* as he called it, gave them great satisfaction.

Chapter Five

They met up a week later and checked over details of the plan Frederick thought up one more time. Frederick addressed the Pirates as if he were a military leader. He went over the key points of the plan, making sure everyone knew their part.

"Okay we know the plan; everything must be done in order so we don't have any hiccups." He looked at Fritz. "Fritz, stand up when I'm talking to you." He paused, all eyes looking at Fritz. "Oh you are, sorry." He grinned. Fritz had been getting short jokes most of his life and always smiled at them when it came from his friends. But if it were anyone outside the group, he would get annoyed to the extent of fighting.

They set off toward Colonel Manfred Von Furz's home. The low fall sun slipped beneath the trees, casting cold shadows on the land. It was dark when they finally arrived at the isolated cottage. Outside, on a newly erected flagpole, flew the distinctive red flag with a large white circle in the center acting as the background for the black swastika.

A chorus of crickets chirped in the tall grass while the group silently gathered to start the attack. Fritz was first to make his move; he circled around to the back of the cottage to wait until he heard the signal.

Helmut was next to move; he took out a heavy brown paper bag from his backpack and slowly crept up to the front porch. He was pretty useless at being stealthy, his shoes crunching loudly on the gravel. The wooden step creaked when he put his foot on it.

Eva, Karl, and Frederick all squirmed in disbelief. Helmut was overweight and clumsy, and it probably wasn't one of their better ideas to use him for the job. But he had insisted in the secret bunker that he plant the first attack.

He placed the bag on the porch in front of the door, took out a box of matches, and set the top part of the bag on fire. His fat little hand thumped three times on the front door. He turned and ran. Unfortunately, he fell down the steps and landed awkwardly in a rose bush, but picked himself up as well as he could and sprinted back to the others. He ducked down just as Colonel Manfred Von Furz opened the front door.

At first he never noticed the burning package. "Hello?" he bellowed.

It took a few more seconds to sink in that no one was at his door, just a package that was on fire.

He gasped, stepped forward, and started stomping on the package. He had no shoes on, just his socks, but he figured he could quickly just stamp it out and he did. It went out quite quick because of the soft wet contents of the bag. His nose soon picked up on the bags contents.

"Swinehund," he shouted. He shouted it again, followed by some curse words. He slowly peeled off his sock, taking care not to get the fresh dog feces on his hands, although some had soaked through his sock. He screamed in anger again. "Swinehund!"

The shouting and commotion was the signal for Fritz who was waiting at the back of the cottage. As soon as he heard the shouting, he started to climb up the back drainpipe and onto the roof. His light athletic body pulled its way up the down pipe effortlessly. He made his way to the chimney, placed a sack over the smoking chimney, and secured it with string.

"Pig Dog, Pig Dog." Helmut laughed as he imitated Colonel Manfred Von Furz. "Actually, it's just dog poo Colonel, not pig poo in the bag." He roared.

"Shhhh, keep down or he'll hear you." Eva giggled.

The Colonel threw his sock out onto his front yard and limped back into his cottage, walking on his heel, so he would not spread the stinking mess throughout. His face glowed red with anger as he made his way to the kitchen sink. He tried lifting his foot up into the sink to wash it off, but had misjudged how over weight he was and was not nimble enough to perform the exercise. He lost his balance and fell. He cursed again as he realized he had now spread some of the muck on his kitchen floor.

Fritz climbed back down from the roof, slid down the drainpipe, and joined the others. Eva set off towards the Colonel's pride and joy. The Mercedes-Benz 770K was in the driveway; one of fewer than 12,000 models that had been made. No one was allowed within ten feet of the car without him barking at him or her, afraid they might put a fingermark on it.

Eva hesitated. She suddenly remembered her brother Luis telling her that the Colonel once beat a Hitler Youth member for making a smudge on the side window with his nose as he peered in to look at the car's interior. It was an extremely nice vehicle and such nice vehicles were rare in the town of Würzburg. She straightened up and took a deep breath. She had a job to do and couldn't let the others see she was frightened. She opened the glass jar of white paint, dipped in her brush, and began her task.

A wheezing sound was heard coming from inside the house. The teenagers gathered around the front gate, ducked down out of sight, and waited. Eva had finished her painting and joined them, and for a few un-nerving minutes there was silence.

"Maybe the smoke killed him?" Helmut whispered. All eyes looked at him in dread. They had never wanted to hurt anyone; this was just a prank. They rolled the rotten eggs they had in their fingers. Frederick knew that some of his chickens had taken to laying eggs in the hedgerows rather than the Chicken Coop; many eggs had been there for months. He also knew how badly they smelt when broken.

The front door burst open and the Colonel staggered out of the smoke filled cottage, coughing. Smoke bellowed around him. His portal figure made a hilarious sight.

Without warning, Fritz started the final assault. He started hurling rotten eggs at the Colonel, the others joining him. One shattered through his window, while others crashed all around him. Karl was a great shot and each egg he threw hit the Colonel. The Colonel crouched down, screaming and cursing at his attackers.

"The yolks on him now," laughed Helmut.

"Looks like he's getting upset; maybe he can't take a yoke," roared Fritz.

"He's cracking up" Frederick grinned. They continued to throw the eggs and make jokes at the Colonel's expense, all of them laughing except for

Karl. Karl grew angrier and threw them harder; he started cursing at the Colonel.

"This is for Berthold, you fat Nazi Pig. This is for sterilizing him," Karl screamed in anger. The others were surprised by his outburst. He was normally very restrained. Berthold was Karl's older brother and at the age of nine, fell in a tank filled with agricultural ammonia that blinded him.

Under The Nazis' new law, any male or female with a disability that could be hereditary would be subject to sterilization. Berthold's blindness was not hereditary. He was just unlucky and had an accident. However, a local magistrate trying to impress some top Nazi officers also ordered Berthold to be sterilized at age sixteen. It angered many townsfolk in Würzburg, but few would stand up to the Nazis and complain. Berthold had taken to playing music after his accident and was known locally as a great pianist. However, after his sterilization by the Nazis he fell into a deep depression, often heard saying he wished he were dead. He hadn't been near a piano since.

Eva put her hand on Karl's shoulder. "Come on Karl, we have to get out of here. We've done enough."

Helmut grinned. "Yep, we just stirred up more trouble than kicking a nest of kamikaze hornets on steroids."

Fritz eyed Karl suspiciously. He liked Eva more than he would dare tell anyone. Most girls in the Würzburg adored Karl, but Eva always acted cool around him and treated him like any other boy. Now she was touching him and speaking softly. Fritz, although he wouldn't admit it, felt slightly jealous.

Chapter Six

News of the attack on the Colonel swept through the town like lightning the next day. Since it was a Saturday, most towns-folk went to the market. The Hitler Youth were spending the weekend with the Air Arm division of the Hitler Youth. The 'Richthofen Airfield' was first used in World War one; it was closed after the first war, but re-opened and renamed after a WW1 fighter ace pilot as a base for the Hitler Youth Air Arm division. They needed more recruits in that division locally so it was an open day; all boys in the village were requested to attend. Karl, Fritz, Helmut, and Frederick wanted no part of it and didn't attend.

The Hitler Youth was made up with various divisions: Air Arm, Naval units, motorized units, and regular army units. The majority of boys enjoyed it; they learned to fly, sail, drive, shoot, and got to spend some weeks off school at training camps. The smaller, more docile, boys were bullied, even by or under the eyes of the youth leaders. They said it built character, kill or be killed, or in this case fight or get bullied.

Also attending the Richthofen Airfield's open day was Artur Axmann. He was the actual head of the Hitler Youth, a high ranking Nazi officer who was also highly decorated and known personally by the German Chancellor, Adolf Hitler. Artur Axmann was one of only two officers who were awarded the highest military medal, the German Order, and survived the war. It was big news that he was at the event in person.

Buildings in the compound had been freshly painted; everything was spick and span for his arrival. Even small rocks that acted as a border between the grass and the sidewalks were painted white. It was a day that Colonel Manfred Von Furz had been looking forward to for weeks. Despite his attack the night before, he had cleaned himself up and put on a fresh uniform. As much as he wanted to forget the incident, an unpleasant cough reminded him of his ordeal. He was still coughing badly when he walked down his driveway to climb into his car. He never bothered to check the other side of his car; after all, who would dare touch it?

The two Hitler Youth boys patrolling the gate never asked him for identification; he was waved in. Colonel Manfred Von Furz was very well known; the last thing the two sixteen-year-olds on the boom gate wanted was to have a run in with him. They lifted the barriers to allow him to drive through. That's when they noticed something written in white paint along side the car. The Colonel sped through too quickly for them to read it.

He parked his car on the edge of the parade ground. He smiled and took a deep breath of fresh air before marching towards the offices. He barked at some of the lower ranking officers regarding the attack on his home and wanted every available Hitler Youth to be out questioning people after the weekend's events. They seemed concerned about his cough as it was quite severe. He exaggerated a little regarding the attack; he said the attackers threw rocks at him, not rotten eggs. The Colonel noticed through an office window a large commotion outside around his car; two youth leaders and a group of boys were pointing at it. He strode out to see what the problem was. Artur Axmann himself was looking at it and pointing.

"Is this your car Colonel?" Artur Axmann asked.

"Heil Hitler," The Colonel said as he saluted and snapped his heels together.

"Heil Hitler. Your car?" Artur Axmann queried with his eyebrows raised.

"Yes sir, very rare. Mercedes-Benz 770K. The Fuehrer himself has the exact same model sir."

"I see." Axmann paused. He slapped his folded gloves into the palm of his hand. "And do you think the Fuehrer would drive it to a Luftwaffe base with this painted on the side of it?" He pointed to the side of the car.

Perplexed and bewildered, the Colonel tentatively walked to the front of his car so he could look at what everyone was staring at.

He read the words 'EDELWEISS PIRATES' in white paint. He immediately touched it to see if he could wipe it off. But it was dry and secure. He knew this would take a huge amount of work to get off and could have damaged his car's finish.

"Swinehund," he screamed. "When I find out who was responsible for this and the attack on my home, they will hang." He described to Axmann the details regarding the attack on his home. While he was explaining about the paper bag, the Colonel would not swear on it, but for the briefest of moments he thought he detected Axmann actually smirk. No! He had to have been mistaken; he would never approve of such behavior.

As far as the Colonel was concerned, the Air-Corp day was ruined. He moved his car to a corner out of sight. He noticed some of the Hitler Youth boy's grinning when they saw it. One Youth, who was fortunate enough to have a camera, even had the nerve to ask the Colonel if he would pose in a picture next to his car. He said he was building a photographic journal of his life as a Hitler Youth. The Colonel made the youth go and clean all the toilets and told him to take a picture of them when they were clean.

It took a local repair shop two days to remove the paint and polish it so no trace of the wording or marks were visible. The same repair shop had to handle another situation caused by the pirates a few days later. Nazi trucks that were parked up outside the train station were also written with the words 'Edelweiss Pirates' and had potatoes stuffed up the exhaust pipes. The build-up of exhaust fumes caused the trucks to stall and refuse to start until the repair shop removed the blockage.

The Nazis did not take such an act of sabotage lightly. Many towns across Germany had a few run-ins with Edelweiss Pirates. Now Wurzburg had the same problem. Frederick and his team had started to make a name for themselves. Little did they know how dangerous the game was that they were now playing.

Chapter Seven

The Pirates planned another attack two weeks later. Eva had learned from her brother Luis that the Hitler Youth would be spending the weekend at Camp Bulge. It was an old WW1 army training facility. Most of the land was now farmed, but the main barracks, some offices, and most of the parade ground was used for Hitler Youth weekends. This week's planned attack by the Edelweiss Pirates was called 'Operation Outhouse.' This was going to be the largest scale attack so far. As usual, Frederick planned it. Everything had to work like clockwork if it was going to be a success. They all knew it carried more risk than anything they had done before. This time they would engage the Hitler Youth.

The Pirates set off for Camp Bulge just after dark on Friday. Frederick and Fritz both carried backpacks full of magnesium sulfate or 'Epsom salts' as it was called. Fritz combed black shoe polish through his blond hair and Frederick did the same to his red hair. Both covered their cheeks in the black polish so they would not get seen in the dark. Eva was wearing a tight dress and carried a pair of high heel shoes; Helmut and Karl also carried a backpack full of surprises. Fritz was happy to be teamed up with Frederick, as they were best friends. Fritz was the only one who could get away with telling him to take a bath when he stunk without getting thumped. Unfortunately, that was most of the time because Frederick did stink, mainly because he helped his grandpa around the farm. Grandpa Gunthrie was not the cleanest person himself, so Frederick never had a good role model. Fritz lived with his aunt; he was also fourteen but many thought he was only twelve because of his small frame and height. Nevertheless, after Frederick, he was the toughest and probably a better athlete than Frederick.

Two sixteen-year-old Hitler Youth boys stood guard at the entrance; they chattered about joining the army when they turned eighteen. One of them wanted to join the Tank regiment; the other wanted to serve under Field Marshal Rommel in Africa. Eva paused opened her bag and changed into her high heels. She let down her blonde hair and walked towards the gate, putting as much sway in her hips as she could. She had seen a Hollywood movie before the war with Hollywood actress Ginger Rogers playing the leading female role. Eva mimicked how Ginger Rogers walked in heels.

"What do we have here?" The two boys beamed.

"Hi guys." She seductively smiled tilting her head to one side. "My brother Luis is staying here this weekend and I made a cake for him and his friends."

"Well that's nice of you. Sorry, but you can't come in." One apologized.

She pouted. "I know there is a war on, but..." She paused, fluttering her eyelashes at them. "Well, maybe you two handsome men can take some and see that he gets the rest." She smiled and raised her eyebrows at them. While the two boys' attention was engaged, Frederick and Fritz tiptoed in the other side of the gate. One of the boys was about to turn and look, but Eva placed her fingers gently on his face and felt his chin. "You guys must shave. How old are you, eighteen?" she asked.

"Em, well, nearly seventeen and yes I shave," he said as he stuck out his chest and beamed, his confidence increasing by the second.

"So do I. I have been for about a year now," the other boy said, not wanting to be outdone. He stuck his chin forward for her to stroke. Eva grinned. She found them both good-looking but reminded herself she was just here to act as a decoy. She opened the cake tin and took out two slices of cake.

Frederick and Fritz ran up to the barracks. The majority of the Hitler Youth had just been given a demonstration on how to clean and breakdown a rifle. They were now being taught how to survive in the wilderness without food and live off the land. They sat in parallel lines one hundreds yards away from the dormitory. A large campfire kept the area lit and warm.

Gingerly, Frederick and Fritz opened the dormitory door. They sneaked inside and started looking up at the ceiling. Once they found the ceiling hatch to the attic they pulled a table under it and put a chair on the table. Fritz kept watch while Frederick climbed up onto the chair and opened the ceiling hatch.

"Fritz, your backpack," Frederick hissed. He put Fritz's pack strap over his arm and lifted himself up in the attic. He took out his matches and lit a small candle he had in his pocket. Slowly, he walked across the cross members towards the water tank. It was much bigger than he had expected. Grandpa told him he would need about one pound of Epsom salts in a large tank to make it work. This tank was massive, so Frederick put his and Fritz's ten-pound bags of Epsom salts into the tank.

"Better be safe than sorry," he thought.

"Quick, someone's coming," Fritz shouted. Without placing the lid back on, Frederick swiftly made his way back across the beams. Fritz was holding the chair steady. "Hurry." Frederick squeezed back down, closed the hatch, and jumped down. They put the chair back and darted into the shower room and hid behind a wall. Two Hitler youth members entered, followed by another two. The boys were the same age as Frederick and Fritz. They were covered in mud and sweat; it soon became obvious to Fritz and Frederick that these guys were going to take a shower. They quickly darted into a toilet cubicle and locked the door. Fritz stood on the seat so they could only see one pair of feet under the door. They heard the showers get switched on and could hear the boys laughing as they showered.

"It's now or never. We got to make a run for it," Frederick whispered. Thinking it was clear, they opened the door and were surprised to see one of the boys naked a few feet away examining a gash on his leg he had suffered while running in the dark.

"Who are you?" the boy asked. Frederick bolted straight at him and punched him, the shock and heavy blow knocking the boy on his back. Fritz followed and stomped on the poor boy on his way past. They burst out of the dormitory and headed down an embankment and out towards the perimeter fence.

Helmut and Karl had gone around the back of Camp Bulge. After the last mission Frederick wanted Helmut to have less of an active role. He knew Karl would keep him out of trouble. They made their way to the edge and started a small fire at the far perimeter of Camp Bulge. They placed a baking tin on the fire and poured on some live bullets they had taken from Grandpa's secret stash. Once the decoy was set they took off over the fields to meet at the rendezvous point.

*

The four Hitler Youths ran out in pursuit of Frederick and Fritz. One had blood raining down his face and held his nose. They yelled for help and soon got the attention of the ninety strong group who sat having a lecture. Included in the group were Colonel Manfred Von Furz and two other Youth leaders. They could just make out Fredrick and Fritz running in the distance being chased by four unclothed boys. Immediately the group started chase, some pulling out their daggers. Adrenaline rushed through the highly testosterone strung youths. "Get them," some cried.

"Edelweiss Pirates," another shouted. Although it was just a guess by the boy who shouted it, the mere mention of the name sent the youths and leaders into a frenzy. It was as if they had kicked a wasp next. Frederick and Fritz had to literally run for their lives.

The first bullet on Karl and Helmut's fire exploded. Some of the boys who were in hot pursuit stopped to look in the direction of the bang, while some kept going. Colonel Manfred Von Furz pulled out his pistol, his eyes darting around the camp. Another bullet exploded, followed by another.

"Halt," the Colonel shouted. "Take cover. We're under attack." He fired his Lugar in the direction of the exploding bullets.

Panic set in across the camp. None of them knew what was happening. Some of the Hitler Youth boys caught the boys who where naked and taking a shower, but without a uniform no one knew who was who. They soon lost interest in Frederick and Fritz, who had now made it to the perimeter fence and started to snip the fence with wire cutters.

"Hurry," Fritz puffed. "Faster. I knew we should have cut this before we went in."

"Shut up and help," Frederick barked.

Eva had already left the love stricken teenage guards with there cake. She made her way back to the rendezvous point where Helmut and Karl were already waiting.

"I think they got caught. The shouting started before the bullets went off," Karl gasped.

"Oh, I hope not. Well, Frederick can fight them off," she said confidently.

"Maybe two or three, but there must have been over one hundred of them and we heard shots from a gun coming from the camp."

"Eva, have you got any cake left?" Helmut asked. Eva and Karl both looked at him and simultaneously said no.

"All right, keep your hair on; I was only asking," replied Helmut. He wouldn't admit it now but thought that it was a waste of good cake.

It took Frederick and Fritz another hour to meet up with them. They had taken a long way around just to be on the safe side. "Damn that was close," Fritz panted.

"Did you put it in the water tank?" Karl asked. Frederick nodded, still trying to catch his breath.

"How much?"

"All of it." He laughed. The others roared with laughter except Fritz.

"It's not funny. We got shot at, attacked, and chased by the new naked division of the Hitler Youth and then by a hundred of them. They wanted blood." He couldn't hold it back anymore he burst out laughing.

Chapter Eight

It was around eight the next morning when the first casualties at Camp Bulge started to use the bathroom. They were up at six for their breakfast of hot tea and toast. This was followed by a morning two-mile jog. When they came back, many drank more water to quench their thirst. The Epsom salts, when taken internally, act as a very strong laxative. The amount Frederick put in the water system would cause severe diarrhea and cramping.

The dormitory only had three toilet cubicles. They were all full and a line started to form. Within an hour they ran out of bathroom paper. Many of them could not hold it and had unfortunate accidents. Some ran to the woods and used leaves or anything else they could find to clean themselves. First it was severe diarrhea, and shortly after came severe stomach cramps, this was followed by dehydration.

The Colonel was also a sufferer. He was forced to slip away in his car after he thought he was going to break wind and regrettably had a loose bowl movement that ended up running down his legs. He quickly drove home to clean up and change his clothing. He came back to find many of the boys in the same predicament. They never had the luxury of going home to change; they had to wash their pants out in the sinks with others. Fortunately for them, everyone was in the same pickle so no one would say anything.

Although the weekend was planned to run until Sunday afternoon, it was cancelled Saturday night. The sewage system eventually became blocked up. With no paper and many of the boys not making it to the bathrooms in time, the stench was overpowering.

A doctor was called out and was concerned the boys would get dehydrated. He ordered them to drink more water. The more they drank, the worse it got. Two boys had to be taken to hospital and would not be released for three days.

Luis was also a sufferer. When Eva saw him clenching his stomach and looking grey she felt sorry for him. He spent most of Saturday night and Sunday in the outhouse. The four boys who discovered Frederick and Fritz were questioned and could only say it was two boys with no particular description; they lied and said they were at least eighteen. They didn't want to look weak and admit that they looked the same age as them and that four of Germany's finest Hitler Youth could not hold two suspected Edelweiss Pirates, especially one that only looked about twelve.

The Colonel ordered an immediate investigation with the official secret police, known simply as the Gestapo. They were feared by many and thought to be almost as ruthless as the protection squad, who were called the SS.

The Gestapo questioned the four boys who were in the showers. They took samples of the water and were able to work out what was used. They started an investigation that led nowhere. They knew it was Epsom salts and tried to see if someone locally had just purchased some. The only store that sold it was a Jewish hardware store and that had been closed down by the Nazis some three months before. The building was burnt to the ground; all records were destroyed.

Going forward, all military bases, be it Army, Navy, Air-force, or Hitler Youth, had the water tanks secured to prevent a recurrence. Unwillingly, the Edelweiss Pirates of Würzburg helped the Third Reich increase security across Europe, something that they would not be proud of.

The Pirates laughed about it when Eva told them what Luis had told her of the consequences. Operation Outhouse had been a huge success as far as they were concerned. Frederick told them that Grandpa had had the Epsom salts for years, so no one would be able to trace it back to them. Luis also told Eva that the culprits were reported to be around eighteen-years- old. This made the investigation run cold.

"We should have called it 'Operation Crap Your Pants.'" Karl laughed. "Or 'Operation don't break wind.'"

"How about 'Operation Chocolate Sauce," Helmut grinned.

"Eewww." Eva cringed, pulling a face as if she was going to be sick. "You boys can be so gross sometimes."

Chapter Nine

After a few days, the incident was forgotten by most. Eva was at home helping her mother prepare dinner.

"Luis, wash your hands and sit with your sister. Dinner is ready," Mrs. Freck told her son. Eva was humming a tune and taping her foot.

"I have to hurry Mother. The Hitler Youth have an important job to do. We have to find those responsible for the attack on Colonel Manfred Von Furz's home and his car," Luis insisted.

"Nonsense, sit and eat first. Your Fuehrer wants you boys to be strong and tough. You need my stew and dumplings in you for that," she tutted.

"Stop humming that stupid tune Eva. That Western jazz music is forbidden," Luis whined.

"'Pennies from Heaven' is a Bing Crosby song. It's not banned," she argued. "Besides, don't order me around. I'm not one of your pocket-sized pretend soldiers that you can march around. If I want to sing, I will." She then started singing 'Swing low, sweet Chariot, coming for to carry me home.' Eva knew it would annoy her brother even more.

"That song *is* banned. It's Western Negro music. If you don't stop I will report you," Luis barked. His father walked into the kitchen and swiftly smacked him across the back of his head.

"You will not report your little sister for singing a song. What is wrong with you and this crazy stuff you talk about?" his father scorned. "Did you hear what the Nazis did to Berthold? They sterilized the poor boy just because of the farming accident. When you were younger you all played together, and now they treat him like he is an animal."

"He is unworthy of life. He is blind. He and his offspring are no use to the fatherland," Luis protested.

"You stupid boy; they have brainwashed you. His offspring will be just as good and healthy as yours. He never had a birth defect. It was a farming accident. What has happened to you Luis? You follow the speeches of this madman like he is god." He grabbed his son's collar to shake him. Luis stared at his father. His eyes watering and lips quivering, he knocked his father's hand away.

"It is righteous, father. You're wrong. I don't mean you any disrespect. You don't attend any of the meetings. Your mind is prejudiced. Do you remember what it was like before the Fuehrer came to power? We had no money, no food. People starved and *you* never had a job. Since he has been in power we are a great nation. You now have a job."

Eva's father looked at Luis. "And at what price does all this come?"

Luis looked away. He turned to Eva and put on a babyish voice. "I know my little sister-poos can't stay angry at big brother Luis. Come on, give me a kiss."

"Don't you dare, Luis," Eva snapped, putting her arms out to stop him. "You stink of sweat."

Luis thought his sister might really blow up if he went with the kiss, so he backed off and gathered his things for tonight's Hitler Youth Meeting. He was still angry about his father's words and ran the two miles. He never stopped running until he reached the Hitler Youth offices.

Eva helped her mother with the dishes. After she finished, she tied up her hair in two ponytails and walked to Frederick's barn. The team had agreed to meet at seven. When she arrived, Fritz and Frederick were playing cards. Karl was winding up a gramophone record player; once he had it fully wound he gently dropped the tone arm on the record. An American jazz band swung into action. Helmut was last to arrive. When he did, he was carrying a large platter covered with a towel.

"Heil Helmut," Frederick saluted, mocking the Nazis who saluted each other the same way. "What have you got there?"

"Mum made an apple strudel for us." Helmut grinned, not sure if he should salute back or not. His gang of friends accepted him; they never judged him for his issues. He ate too much, he was very quiet, and he was very close to his mother. They had all known him since kindergarten and that was just the way Helmut was.

"What, no sausage?" Eva joked, knowing it was Helmut's favorite food.

"I ate it all for dinner." He grinned rubbing his swollen potbelly. "I also ate Fritz's favorite cake." They looked at Helmut puzzled. Fritz was the first to ask.

"How do you know what my favorite cake is?

"I don't. I just assumed it's *short* cake," Helmut teased. The others started laughing.

"Oh we got jokes today, eh Helmut? Come on, no more short jokes," Fritz protested.

"I agree with Fritz; no more jokes about his size. He's getting upset. Must have a *short* fuse tonight." Frederick roared.

"It was only a *little* joke Fritz," Helmut grinned.

They eventually settled down, stopped tormenting Fritz, and started to talk about the attack on the Colonel's cottage and attack at Camp Bulge. They laughed as they recalled the events. The Hitler Youth was out in force looking for groups of youths who had broken the law and refused to join the ranks. Even girls now had to join the League of German Girls in Hitler Youth. Just by refusing to join could mean being sent to a concentration camp.

At sixteen Luis Freck was two years older than his sister Eva. He had drifted apart from her over the last few years. He did not approve of her hanging around with a group of boys who did not seem interested in the future of Germany. He arrived at Hitler Youth in time for inspection that even included feet examination. The Hitler Youth had to learn hygiene and this started with clean feet. They couldn't be expected to march onto victory if they suffered from bad feet or infections.

Tonight they were shown a short movie called 'The Eternal Jew.' The film depicted the Jewish people as filthy, evil, corrupt, and intent on world domination. Next they sat in a classroom and were asked by a youth leader if they had anything to report. They were to inform if they heard a teacher, neighbor, or even family member was involved in unlawful activity.

Luis was tempted to inform them what his father had said about Hitler being a madman and his sister singing banned songs. He wanted to. He knew it would make his leaders proud and it's what he should do but hesitated. Despite her faults, he loved his sister. He would hate to think of what might happen to her if she was taken away to a concentration camp. And if he told on his father, he would be taken away, probably beaten and put in prison. How would his mother cope with that? No, for now he would say nothing. He felt wrong for not revealing the information, but felt better for it. After all, they were family he told himself.

*

The following week, the Hitler Youth, under orders of the Third Reich, started a vicious campaign of attacks on Jewish families. Windows were broken, household items were stolen, children were beaten by older boys, some homes where even torched. It was now forbidden for anyone to use a Jewish business. Many families starved as money ran short. The only synagogue in Würzburg was burned to the ground. The Rabbi had tried to put out the flames. When one of the Hitler Youth saw this, he called him a dirty Jew and struck him over the head with an iron pipe. The Rabbi later died from smoke inhalation and, despite many witnesses, no one was charged for the attack. The police and the Gestapo did nothing regarding the attacks. If anything, it was welcomed. This increased the attacks and made them an easy target for bullies and thieves.

Across Germany the Hitler Youth continued to grow in numbers. In contrast, the Edelweiss Pirates' numbers remained the same. It was harder for them to meet without being seen in a group. Frederick's barn was the perfect location for the Würzburg group of Edelweiss Pirates. He wanted to reach out to other groups but had no means of contacting others. As far as he knew, his small group was the only group in Wurzburg. He knew that even if someone wanted to join his group it would be very difficult for them to join. It wasn't something you could advertise or put up a notice of where they were meeting. He was hoping on meeting some new members at the town dance.

Friday night they met up in the barn and sat around merrily drinking Grandpa's coffee and telling jokes. They never knew how Grandpa Gunthrie could get hold of so much coffee, but all agreed it was better not to ask. Most Germans had to drink 'Ersatz.' a disgusting drink made from ground acorns because Germany was at war with all coffee producing countries.

Grandpa Gunthrie pulled the strap of his piano accordion over his shoulder and played a long note before starting to play a tune. Eva and Helmut started to sing along. Eventually Karl and Fritz joined in. Grandpa Gunthrie paused and looked at Frederick.

"Come, come Frederick sing the song you wrote," he ordered.

Frederick blushed. His normally white face turned crimson, just like his hair. He chewed on his bottom lip and gave his grandpa a filthy look. He had been rehearsing his song, but was a little shy about actually doing it. He took out a jotter book and pulled out some pages and passed them around.

"This is a song I wrote for the Edelweiss Pirates," he murmured.

We are going to write it on the walls and roof
Down, down with the Hitler Youth
The Edelweiss Pirates of Würzburg are we
Hitler & Nazis can drink our pee
We know your rules but hate the game
At least now you know our name
Hitler you may think you're the perfect one
But Edelweiss Pirates have just begun

"It's wonderful," Eva beamed. Everyone else agreed, much to the relief of Frederick. They spent the rest of the evening learning the song. They settled on a tune and made it their theme song.

On the way back home, Eva, Fritz, Helmut, and Karl were singing it when they encountered the unpleasant but familiar sight of a Hitler Youth on patrol. The patrol was made up of ten boys aged between fourteen and sixteen years old, wearing the ridiculous white knee socks, camel colored shorts, and shirt with swastika armbands. Fortunately they saw them and had stopped singing before they were heard.

"Heil Hitler. Where are you going?" the tallest boy aggressively asked as they surrounded them.

"Home. Unless you boys are inviting us to a party?" Eva smiled. Two of the Hitler Youth boys held back a smirk.

"We do not *party*. There is a war on. Where have you been? You know we have been looking for the Edelweiss Pirates. Do you know anyone who is a member?" the tall Hitler Youth quizzed.

"Maybe they are the Edelweiss Pirates?" another Hitler Youth questioned. Fritz was sure he recognized him from school.

"Never heard of them. We have to get home. Good night," Helmut said. He tried to carry on walking but a stocky built Hitler Youth blocked his path.

"Where are you going, fatty?" The stocky member barked. He placed his hand on Helmut's shoulder. Fritz took a few steps forward. He stuck his chest out and eyed the stocky youth. Despite his shorter size, he would normally welcome a fistfight, but knew they were out numbered ten against four and that's if he included Eva. The Hitler Youth had a rigorous training schedule. Their sports activities included boxing. Fritz knew they where tough, but was not about to be bullied by anyone.

"Take your hands off him. We're going home. We don't know any Edelweiss Pirates. We're not Jews. Let us pass." Fritz ordered, his voice hoarse and a little shaky.

Fritz wasn't sure which one of the Hitler Youth gave the order. He heard one of them shout, "Get em." And the next thing he knew he was punched on the side of his face. Karl kicked at the youth but was soon out numbered. Helmut was trying to fend off two attackers. Eva was not spared; she was punched in the face. The blow broke her tooth. When she fell she was repeatedly kicked. Fritz stood his ground and gave back as good as he got. The short small-framed boy fought bravely against the larger boys. Karl was next to fall. He rolled up in a ball to protect his face and body. Helmut was head butted; it knocked him unconscious. Although. Even after he was down and out, he was still not spared from being kicked.

Fritz was eventually held in a headlock. His arms were held behind his back and he felt his nose explode in blood as he was given a severe beating. They continued to pummel him until he was eventually kicked in the groin. He groaned and crumpled into a heap. Crying out in pain, he felt helpless as his body was kicked over and over. It would be several more minutes before the onslaught of kicks and punches stopped, and only then because all ten Hitler Youths were exhausted. They left the small group lying in the road bleeding and in pain, and then marched off triumphantly.

"Agh.... ouch, where is Frederick when you need him?" Karl groaned holding his stomach.

They painfully helped each other up. Eva was shrieking Helmut's name, trying to get him to come around. Gently, she tapped his cheeks. "Helmut, Helmut wake up," she shrieked. Karl shook Helmut.

Fritz, despite his nose pouring blood, bent down and tried to pick Helmut up.

"My god, he's heavy. I can't lift him on my own. Karl help lift him over my shoulder," Fritz grunted. Eva tore a strip off the bottom of her Petty coat and placed it over Fritz's face.

"Ouch," he screamed.

"Sorry Fritz, but you have to stop the bleeding or else you'll pass out. Then we'll have to carry you." Eva started to cry. It was a pathetic spectacle to see the once proud group of friends crying, unconscious, and covered in blood in a country lane. Just when things couldn't get worse it began to rain. The water brought Helmut around. He looked at Eva looking over him. She had blood on her face, her nose and eye swollen, snot running down her nose, and her hair wet, matted and covering part of her face.

"Eva, you look beautiful." he smiled.

"What?" she said, looking at Fritz and Karl who were both kneeling down beside her trying to lift Helmut.

"Yeah, your new look is very fetching." Fritz smiled, still holding the rag on his nose. "What do you think Karl?" Karl looked at Eva's face.

"Oh yes. Very hot Eva. Will you dance with me at the Wurzburg dance?" Karl grinned. The group all burst out laughing. Groaning in pain, they helped

Helmut up from the wet ground. The more they moaned and groaned the more they laughed.

"Now where were we?" Fritz said. "Ah yes…. We are going to write it on the walls and roof," He sang.

The others all joined in and sang it loudly. "Down, down with the Hitler Youth."

They continued to sing the song and walked Eva home. She leaned forward and hugged all three of them. When she hugged Fritz she smoothed the back of his hair, the touch of her fingers and closeness, stirring interesting reactions in his battered body.

Karl coughed. "Well, we better let you get inside Eva. Have your mother look at your injuries." She nodded and slowly walked to her door, briefly glancing at her battered friends before she went inside.

"Eva what happened to you dear?" her mother cried as Eva staggered into her home, barely able to focus through her tear-stained eyes. Her mother escorted her to the sink.

"What happened? Is she okay?" her father replied, climbing out of his chair. Luis came down the stairs. Feeling comforted, Eva let her emotions out and started to cry uncontrollably.

"I bet it was one of those rough boys you hang around with. Did he touch you anywhere? Which one was it? No one does that to my sister," Luis growled. Eva turned and faced him, her emotions switched from crying and feeling sorry for herself to rage. She hurled herself at him, grabbing his shirt collar and shaking him.

"It was not one of my friends, you stupid pig. They're hurt far worse than me. Helmut was almost killed. It was a group of your Hitler Youth friends. We did nothing wrong. We were walking along minding our own business. They kicked and beat us.," she screamed. Her mother took her arms and hugged her. Luis was speechless.

"So, son. Your Hitler Youth group thinks it's good to hurt German children now? What's next, are you going to shoot your mother if dinner is late? Or maybe we should take her outside and stone her if she doesn't iron your shirt the way you like. I told you the Nazis have you brainwashed. They should be fighting the British, not our own children.," their father yelled.

"I... I will find out. Sorry Eva. I would never harm you. Are you sure it was Hitler Youth and not that group, the Edelweiss Pirates?" Luis asked.

"Nonsense, the Pirates only attack the Nazis not the German people. They're on the side of good, against the evil." his father told him. Luis took a step back and eyed his father. Such speech was treason and something he should report to his leaders at Hitler Youth.

"Father, I know you're angry because of Eva, but you mustn't speak like that again. I beg of you," Luis pleaded.

His father placed his trembling hands on his son's shoulders. "Son. Listen to yourself. Are you saying it's wrong for a man to speak his own mind, in his own home, with his family? Look how my only daughter has come home. She and her young friends have been severely beaten. You and I both know nothing will be done to these bullies and yet you lecture me on what I can and cannot say out of frustration."

"No, Papa. But it is forbidden to speak of such things. We have to be strong, for the good of the fatherland. We must fight and rid ourselves of weakness and the Jewish plague." It was what he had heard over and over again at Hitler Youth evenings and camp. The constant propaganda had sunk in to Luis's young mind. To him, it was right. He was very proud to be a German Hitler Youth member.

"Jewish Plague? They are good people, no different from us," Eva wept.

Luis bit his lip before giving a reply. "Eva, you're too young to remember. It was the Jews that declared war on Germany in 1933. From all over the world they boycotted our goods and businesses. They want to put our great county back in bad times," Luis argued.

"Children, please stop this," their mother interrupted. "If Luis wants to join the Hitler Youth to train to be a German officer, then I'm proud of him. Luis, you are our son and we love you. When you are older you will understand. Your views are very welcome here and I enjoy listening to you talk about the Third Reich. But you must observe the same respect for your father and his views."

Luis wanted to storm out of the room. He believed his mother was wrong. It was treason to speak ill of the Nazi party or the Fuehrer. But at least for now, because he felt guilty about how his sister had been treated, he said nothing.

Chapter Ten

Grandpa Gunthrie smiled and rolled on the balls of his feet as he waited for the back door of Otto's home to open. Otto was a wealthy man, a writer and musician. The door opened and a hand gestured him in.

"You will like what I brought you today Otto." Grandpa coughed. He placed an old sack full of goods on the kitchen table and dug his hand in to pick out something.

"Look at these beauties." Grandpa smiled as he gently caressed a bag of eggs, packed with straw. "Most of them double yolkers I bet." He gingerly placed them on the table and dug his hand in again. "Ham, about 4 kilos this beauty weighs." He lifted out a large piece of ham, still attached to the bone.

Otto nodded and smiled. "Gunthrie you have no idea how much I will enjoy that. Anything else?" he questioned with his eyebrows raised.

Grandpa paused. "Well, I do, but it's expensive. I'm, not sure if you can afford this." He slowly pulled out a bottle of French champagne and a block of cheese. "Now, I don't come by this everyday, you know."

Otto walked over to the corner of his room, he pushed a chair away from the wall, lifted a rug, and started to remove some floorboards. He pulled out a box and carried it over to the table.

"DuPont, what's that?" Grandpa asked. Otto pulled out several of the packages and opened one.

"American-made nylon stockings. I can guarantee that no one else in Germany has them." Otto smirked.

The men negotiated the food for several packs of the nylon stockings and some of Otto's Cuban cigars and shook hands. Grandpa's next stop was the local tavern house. There he spent most of the afternoon drinking for free in exchange for a single pair of nylons for the landlady.

He noticed a poster on the tavern wall. There was to be a dance on Saturday at the village hall. To Grandpa Gunthrie, that meant an opportunity to sell his nylons for a nice profit or good barter. Any woman going would love to be the only person at the dance with real nylons.

On his way home the local policeman, Rolf, stopped him. Grandpa immediately sobered up and came alert. "Evening Rolf. How are you on this fine afternoon?"

Rolf eyed him and his sack suspiciously. "Heil Hitler," he stamped. "I'm well, thank you Gunthrie. I see you've been drinking. I wonder how you get the money to buy beer. And I wonder what you have in the sack."

Grandpa squirmed and stuttered. "I have been saving up. It's just my dirty laundry in the sack. If you want to look at my underwear you're welcome, but I have to warn you, it's not pleasant. I've had some stomach problems and can't always get to the bathroom."

Rolf kept walking. "I'm too busy to fuss with you now. There's a war on, you know. I'm still trying to catch the vandals who attacked Colonel Manfred Von Furz. He's a veteran; he fought in the first Great War. Flew in a Zeppelin, he did. How people could treat a war hero like this is just treason. But mark my words, I will find them."

"Don't hold your breath." Gunthrie smiled to himself.

Chapter Eleven

A dark cloud hung over Luis's head the next morning on his way to school. He was angry about what his father had said, but far worse was seeing Eva this morning with a painful black eye and bruised face, He was determined to find out who was responsible for the outrageous attack on his little sister and her friends.

At morning break he made his way to the schoolyard and to a group of boys he had suspected may have been responsible. He found them gathered in a group in the corner. He walked into the center of the group.

"Hail Hitler," he saluted. In return they all saluted back, although it was not often done at school unless you wanted to prove or pretend you were more loyal than others to the Fuhrer. He noticed Erwin had a cut above his eye and nose was swollen. This confirmed his suspicions.

"Erwin, what happened to your face?" Luis questioned. His voice rang out with authority. He looked deep into Erwin's eyes; it was slightly un-nerving for the tall youth.

"Ha, we met some scruffy locals, last night. Had to teach them a lesson and what the Hitler Youth can do." Erwin grinned, although he took a step back, because his space was invaded.

"Ya, probably 'wanna be' Edelweiss Pirates; they had a girl too," Another piped up.

"So, when did we start beating up locals for fun and hitting girls? We're Hitler Youth, not bullies." Luis spat. The others picked up on his aggression and knew there was more to the story.

After a pause it was Erwin who spoke first. "Are you getting soft, Luis?"

"Soft? So you think it makes you hard to beat children and girls? You out numbered them in age and numbers and you think I'm soft. God help the fatherland, if you, Big Tall Erwin are ever on the front line and a Tommy comes face to face with you, I mean a real Tommy, one of Churchill's soldiers not a teenage girl." Luis spat his words.

The inevitable fistfight started. Luis hit Erwin in the stomach, but was surprised when Erwin recoiled and came back at him so fast, kicking wildly with his legs and flailing fists. The crowd soon gathered and could be heard whooping as the two boys wrestled each other in headlocks, punching, kicking, and even biting each other. But just as inevitable as the fight was the meeting in the head master's office after, where both bruised and battered boys each received six strokes of the cane for fighting.

On his way home from school, the past events went around inside Luis's head. Something was bugging him, but he couldn't quite put his finger on it. An uneasy feeling snaked around his insides. He stepped onto the grass bank to allow a car to pass him along the narrow lane. It was Colonel Manfred Von Furz in his Mercedes-Benz 770K. Luis was left in a cloud of exhaust fumes, and then he remembered. Just before the fight, one of the group called Eva and her friends a wanna be Edelweiss Pirates group'.

Luis thought for a while. What if they are Edelweiss Pirates? Come to think of it, most of her friends like her must be fourteen now or very nearly. Why weren't they in the Hitler Youth? It troubled him. If he was right, she was in grave danger. The Gestapo was getting tougher on rebels like Edelweiss Pirates. Just last week a seventeen-year-old boy was hung in Frankfurt for distributing Edelweiss Pirates leaflets and propaganda. Luis knew he had to have it out with Eva. He also knew she would of course deny it.

When he arrived home he kissed his mother on the cheek and rushed upstairs to his room to change into his Hitler Youth uniform. He had heard that some of them would be getting new daggers. His and others had become damaged because of the amount of times they threw them into a tree trunk in a game of target. His mother called him to come down to dinner.

Eva was helping to serve dinner. It was a stew that consisted of boiled potatoes, turnip, onion, and sausage. He sat and glanced at Eva. She noticed his stare and looked away.

"Your face looks better today Eva, the bruising has gone down." He smiled.

"Yours looks worse. I heard about the fight in school." She paused and looked at him. "Thank you, but you shouldn't get hurt on my account." Eva gently tapped the back of her brother's hand. It was a small gesture but it meant a lot. They often fought as brother and sister, but deep down they loved each other.

"Luis, Eva, did you hear about your cousin Katharina? She will be able to pay another two hundred and fifty Marks off her marriage loan. She is hoping this time it's a boy." Their mother grinned, pulling the bread roll apart.

"I don't understand how that whole marriage loan thing works. Does she get it for every baby and the medal? Eva asked frowning.

"If you join Hitler Youth, you would learn such things." Luis interrupted. "When you get married you get a one thousand marks as a loan if the woman gives up work and stays home. Every child you have within six years two hundred and fifty marks gets paid off. So if you have four children your loan is paid off and you get a Bronze Mother's Iron Cross medal."

"I thought it was something like that. They can keep their thousand marks. When I get married, I'll have children when I want them and probably only two, like us," Eva said.

"Then you won't get a Mother's Cross," Luis argued. "We need more German people, so we should have more children." Luis spoke like he was making a speech. Eva mimicked a yawn as if she was bored.

After dinner Eva met up with the boys at the barn. Because of the beating they had suffered their spirits were down. Frederick tried to liven things up; he put a record on the gramophone. They sat quietly and enjoyed the music but did not sing along or dance around. They still suffered from bruises. Fritz had two cracked ribs and found it very uncomfortable to breath.

"Maybe we should just go home?" Helmut suggested. Normally Helmut was a follower and never suggested much. As long as he had food in his mouth he was happy. "I know what's wrong. Where is Grandpa Gunthrie?"

Frederick glumly spoke. "A pig at the Wolfgang farm died of pneumonia. That's like Christmas and ten birthdays all rolled into one for

Grandpa. I guess we'll all be eating pork this week."

Farms across Europe were under strict control. An inspector would come around every week or so and count the livestock. Food was rationed, so a farmer could not simply slaughter an animal and feed his own family. That was a crime, not only in Germany, but also in most countries. It carried a fine and small prison sentence.

Grandpa Gunthrie had a trick up his sleeve and all the local farmers knew about it. It was the farm inspectors who where kept in the dark.

When the farmer discovered his pig had died of pneumonia he contacted the inspector and Grandpa Gunthrie. The inspector would visit the farm immediately, look over the dead animal, and reduce the amount of pigs held by one. The farmer would then dispose of the dead animal by burning or burying it. However, Grandpa Gunthrie would collect it on his cart, pay the farmer a few bottles of wine, and go to another farm that had pigs.

He would put the dead pig in the pigpen, after which that farmer called out the inspector. The inspectors didn't recognize the fact they had already seen the same pig a few hours before and reduce the pig count by one on that farm. That now meant the farmer can slaughter a good pig and sell the meat and feed his family. Of course Grandpa Gunthrie was given a large joint of pork and sometimes eggs and milk for his trouble. He would use the same pig for about four or five farms. Each time he would either hose off the dead pig or roll it in the mud of the pigpen to make it look slightly different. He got imaginative and placed it in various positions.

*

Grandpa Gunthrie worked through the night and most of Saturday morning. When he came home he was stinking of sweat and pig poo, even he thought he always smelt bad.

"Grandpa you stink." Frederick winced as he strolled into the kitchen carrying his best shirt.

"That's the smell of money and good food, my boy. You won't be complaining when you're eating freshly cooked pork or home made cake. And I will be getting some chocolate." He wheezed. "Yeah, you're right I do smell a bit. I have been in pig poo all night. I'm going to the baths today."

"I'm going later when I have finished the milking. I'm going to the dance tonight." Frederick grinned.

"Here's two deutschmarks. That's enough for the baths and in case you want to get that girl Eva flowers," Grandpa smiled begrudgingly, passing over the money.

Frederick snatched it. "Thanks, Grandpa, but Eva is not my girlfriend. We are just friends."

Chapter Twelve

Würzburg public baths were housed in a two-century-old building that used to be a monastery. For just one Pfennig you could take a hot bath and use the steam room, it was another one Pfennig for a clean towel. It was sectioned off for males and females, although children under ten would normally bathe in the female section. Many homes never had a bathroom, just an outhouse. However, most did have a tin bath that could be set up in the kitchen and filled with water from pans and a kettle.

Helmut was like most fourteen-year-old boys. He felt he was too old to bathe in the house in front of his mother so he had taken to going to the baths once a week. He had taken a hot bath and strolled into the steam room. It was a dimly lit room, full of steam provided by a hot furnace. He sat on a large tiled ledge and closed his eyes. The room had about fifteen other users, mostly older men. Saturday was the most popular day for the men to bath/ Sundays were popular for children. Parents wanted the kids clean before the week's schooling.

"Ah Helmut, my boy. I guess you're going to the party tonight as well." It was Grandpa Gunthrie.

He sat next to Helmut and wiped the sweat that had already started to form on his brow. Helmut opened his eyes and strained to make him out in the steam.

"You have good eye sight if you could make me out in the steam.," Helmut smiled.

"Well, I saw your bicycle outside and you're the only boy in here. I knew that it must have been you." Grandpa smiled. "Plus, like me you carry a little extra insulation on your bones." He joked as he rubbed his fat stomach.

"We'll get black snow tomorrow. Is this your yearly bath?" Helmut teased.

"Enough of your cheek young feller. I've been busy, up all-night."

They both relaxed and were soon joined by Frederick. He sat between them. The two boys discussed what girls would be going to the party. Grandpa got up and slowly made his way to the door, being careful not to slip on the wet floor.

A few minutes later and the familiar large naked shape of Grandpa Gunthrie returned. He sat down next to the boys.

"Grandpa, so when will we be eating pork? It's been months since we had any," Frederick asked.

"Yes, I want some too. My mum has a bottle of vodka. She doesn't drink and says she wanted to trade it for a joint," Helmut asked.

The large naked shape looked at the two boys. "Pork. Are you calling me a pig or are you talking about black market goods?" It was Colonel Manfred Von Furz. In the steam his outline was identical to Grandpa Gunthrie's. Both boys sat up and strained their eyes through the steam. Once they realized who it was they quickly got up.

"We weren't talking to you, sir. We're rehearsing a play. Sorry if we bothered you," Helmut stuttered. "Well I got to go, Frederick or I'll pass out. It's so hot in here today."

Colonel Manfred Von Furz eyed the boys suspiciously. "I don't know you boys. Why are you not in the Hitler Youth?"

"We are both thirteen, sir. Next year we are both going to join," Frederick lied.

"You could both join the DJ." He questioned. The DJ stood for Deutsches Jungvolk, German Young People. It was for boys ten to thirteen, but was not compulsory like the Hitler Youth was. They found it easier to lie about their age. "Also, your hair is too long. You look like hooligans. The Hitler Youth will straighten you boys up."

"We could, but we don't want to. Anyway, I got to go as well; it's hot in here. Nice talking to you, sir. I'll come with you Helmut," Frederick croaked. Both boys left the steam room and took a cold plunge bath. Once they had cooled off, they saw the funny side and started laughing.

"I thought it was my Grandpa." Frederick laughed. "He has the same Dicky Do.

"Dicky Do?" Helmut quizzed as he dried himself.

"Yeah, his belly sticks out more than his *dicky do*." Frederick laughed. "Mind you, Helmut, if you keep eating sausage you'll get a Dicky Do, too." Helmut did not see the funny side and rolled his towel up and flicked Fredericks back with it. Both boys sparred trying to flick their towels at each other, giggling and screaming like six-year-old girls when the tip of the towel whipped their flesh.

Eva dressed quite plainly for the party. Her parents were pleasantly surprised when she came down the stairs. A few months ago, they had all had an argument about a skirt she wanted to wear. Her father said it was much too short and she had undone two top buttons from the neck down. Today she dressed very conservatively and in a manner that her father approved of. As she was leaving, she picked up a small bag of grey and black ash she had scooped up from the fireplace earlier that day.

Carrying the bag of ash like it was gold dust. She walked two miles to meet her only female friend, Gretchen. They had been friends since kindergarten, although in the past year or so they had drifted apart. Gretchen had joined the League of German Maidens, the female version of the Hitler Youth. She was still annoyed that Eva hadn't also joined when she turned fourteen. Eva made excuses, none of which were believed.

Gretchen screamed in delight when she saw Eva arrive. Her mother worked as a waitress at the hotel so she was alone in the house. Both girls grinned and ran to the kitchen. Eva collected a bowl and poured in the ash, being careful not to make a cloud of dust. Meanwhile, Gretchen sliced up a beetroot and placed it in a bowl. Using the potato masher, she crushed the beetroot. They grinned wickedly as they worked.

Eva's short dress was already at Gretchen's house. She had taken it there during the week after sneaking it out of the house. Once dressed in clothing that two fourteen-year-old girls thought was more suitable for a dance, they went down stairs to put the final part of their plan together. Eva stood on a stool and lifted the back of her skirt up.

"Do make sure it's straight." She grinned.

Gretchen had her mother's eyeliner black pencil. It was the only make-up her mother had, but rather than apply to there eyes, each girl drew a straight line up the back of each leg. Once the line was drawn, the grey ash was rubbed over legs, ankles, and feet. Nothing was missed, even the toes where given a covering of the dirty grey ash. Eva did the same for Gretchen. They slipped on their shoes and both climbed onto the kitchen table so they could view their legs in the large mirror that hung over the kitchen stove.

"Perfect." Eva smiled. "They look like real stockings. No one will know." The eyeliner looked like the seam.

Gretchen beamed as she looked at herself in the mirror. "Now for the final trick."

Using a tiny brush, she applied the mashed beetroot to her lips. The dark red liquid stained their lips, to give the impression of lipstick. The girls' final trick was to place a sock in each cup of their bras to give the impression of a larger size. After a final grooming, both girls set off on foot to the town center's village hall.

Karl pulled on his jacket and found himself looking in the mirror: fair hair, blue eyes, freckles, and a slim pale face. The bruising around his cheek was too pronounced to ignore.

"I don't think you're going to be able to hide those bruises. The girls of Wurzburg are in a treat tonight, Karl. You look so grown up, like your father had thirty years ago." His mother smiled lovingly, brushing the back of his jacket with her hand. "And I expect Eva will be there?"

"Mother, we are just friends. She is one of the gang; we hang out together." He blushed.

"Ah hum, I see the way you look at her, I know *that* look." She grinned and kissed his cheek. "Have a nice time."

Karl spent a few minutes with his older brother Berthold before leaving. He said he would tell

Berthold everything that happened when he got back. He asked again if Berthold wanted to go, he could sit and listen to the music, but just as Karl expected he declined. Karl often spent time with his blind older brother. Since his sterilization by the Nazis, Berthold had been in a deep depression and very rarely left the house.

Karl tried to keep him up to date with events. He had noticed that Berthold had been very interested in the Edelweiss Pirate actives. When Karl told him the details of Operation Outhouse it was the first time in months he heard his brother laugh. Berthold wanted desperately to help but was unable to because of his blindness.

Chapter Thirteen

A large majority of the town turned up to the dance. During wartime any event like this helped them take the tragedies off their minds, even if it was only for a short period. Hitler Youth members wore their uniforms and stood in groups around the side of the dance floor. They dared each other to ask a girl to dance. The girls were also congregated in small groups as well and giggled if they thought the boys where looking at them.

Helmut, Frederick, Fritz, and Karl had other plans. They were going to ask the young ladies to dance. Being older there was always the chance of making out with them. With most of the men away at war, it was the perfect opportunity for the fourteen-year-olds to expand their experiences with the opposite sex. Although all four boys were the same age, Fritz would not be able to act older, despite his mature nature. He looked younger than his years. He was still suffering from his injuries, but shrugged them off.

Eva walked in with Gretchen. As they strolled across the dance floor, heads followed them. The boys had to take a second look at Eva. They were used to seeing her in a long skirt and leather jacket. It was obvious she was growing into a young lady.

Fritz nudged Karl. "Karl look, she has legs."

"And..... You know, she's also got toys." Helmut grinned as he Karl, Fritz, and Frederick ogled her figure with gaping mouths.

"Wow Eva you look. Em, nice." Frederick stuttered. "But you have the Hitler Youth boys looking you up and down."

"Let them look," Gretchen interrupted. Eva said nothing; she wouldn't dance with them, but secretly she was enjoying the attention she was getting.

"Eva you have something in your eye," Fritz smiled.

"Which one?" She asked looking at him.

"Oh no, it's just a sparkle." He grinned. "Can I get you anything? Tea, coffee, me?" he asked with his eyebrows raised, revealing his blue eyes.

"Well you get ten out of ten for trying Fritz." She laughed, much to the annoyance of Karl. He thought he should compliment her, but the words just never came straight away.

"This music sucks. I'm gonna see if they will play some of my records." Karl announced. He went across and spoke to Mr. Erikson who was playing German brass band music records. "Mr Erikson, no one is dancing, your music is..." He paused. "Well it's very nice sir, but the crowd is much younger here. The dance floor is deserted. It's as quiet as a queen's fart! Can you play some of my records?" he said, passing a bag containing four vinyl records.

"This is Beethoven. He's the world's greatest composer. It has a great rhythm to dance to. But I agree it is like a... well I won't say what you said young man. Oh very well. Is it legal music?" Mr. Erikson asked. He had purposely left his glasses at home, in hope of getting a dance with one of the ladies, in particular Fraulein Weissmuller, the kindergarten head mistress. He squinted but could not read the label.

"Oh yes sir. I'm in the Hitler Youth. We play these at meetings," Karl lied. The first record was 'Sing Sing Swing (With a swing)' by American jazz bandleader Benny Goodman. As soon as it started with its persuasive foot tapping drum solo, the Edelweiss Pirates took to the dance floor. Some of the girls joined them. Hitler Youth members held themselves back, but couldn't help tapping their feet to the influential addictive beat. In less than a minute the dance floor was packed with the youngsters dancing swing style. Mr Erikson seemed concerned but was enjoying the music and everyone seemed happy.

Karl moved in on Eva. "Will you dance with me?" He took her hand before she had time to think about it. "Eva you're gonna give me toothache." He laughed.

"Why?"

"It's just, you're so sweet." He grinned. Eva enjoyed the attention she was getting. Karl's fun was short lived. After three dances Fritz cut in. For the next hour they played Karl's records over and over again. Fritz and Karl both took turns dancing with Eva every few songs.

Then the main doors were thrown open. All eyes looked as Colonel Manfred Von Furz appeared. He marched across the dance floor shadowed by two Hitler Youth and a policeman. He took the record off the player and snapped the records in half. Karl was furious. Fritz held him back. Luis was one of the Hitler Youth.

"Don't Karl, keep in the crowd," Fritz told him. Helmut stepped in as well and held him back. Helmut's face was bright red. He was quite unfit, but had got carried away dancing.

"You are under arrest," the Colonel barked to Mr. Erikson. "This noise and that type of dancing is outlawed." He turned and faced the crowd. "Those of you who were dancing will give your names before you leave. We shall be speaking to you later."

"It's not my music. It's the Hitler Youth's music. That boy gave me the records to play." Mr. Erikson objected, pointing at Karl. The Colonel's eyes darted in Karl's direction. Luis looked as well and noticed them trying to calm Karl down. It was obvious to Luis that Mr. Erikson was telling the truth. Just as he focused on Karl the air raid sirens went off.

"The shelters," someone shouted. A few girls screamed. They had been through a couple of air raids before, but had been at home with family. Being away from home caused some to panic. The Colonel tried to get his voice heard above the noise and the siren, but his voice was lost in a sea of screams and shouts. No one stopped to give their names. They started pouring out of the building and making their way to various shelters. Some made it home where they had shelters built in basements or under stairs.

The Pirates lived in the country. It was too far to go home for shelter, so Frederick took charge as he always did. He led his friends to Fortress Marienberg. Below the Fortress was a stone bridge. He took them under the huge brick arches. It was bitterly cold under the bridge, but after dancing and running for shelter they welcomed the cold night air.

"Is this safe?" Fritz asked.

"This has been around longer than my grandpa. It's gotta be safe. Those dirty pig Tommies have nothing that could blow up this bridge. It was built in 704 AD," Frederick scoffed.

"It might be the Yanks," Fritz replied. "I heard they were joining in against us now. But the Japs put them in their place, blew up one of their navy fleets in Hawaii just before Christmas at Diamond Harbor I think they called it?"

"Pearl Harbor," Eva replied. They all stared at Eva, surprised she knew the name.

"Don't look at me like that, just because I'm a girl," she barked. "My dad and Luis argue about the news all the time so it's hard not to learn stuff." she grinned.

"Anyone got some food?" Helmut asked.

The first bombs started to fall before he could get an answer; Frederick put his arm around Eva to comfort her. The sky was lit up with searchlights and anti-aircraft rounds. Huge explosions rocked the town. With each crack and bang came a terrific gust of wind. All they could hear was the constant whistling as the bombs fell, then the explosion as it hit its target.

The roar of the British Lancaster bombers became deafening as they dropped down, flying over rooftops for a machine-gun attack. People ran in all directions desperately trying to get out of the path of the bullets that crossed the main street. Most bounced off the cobblestones and ricocheted at all angles, but still retaining enough force to kill or seriously injure. Direct hits pounded the rooftops, a horse and buggy, and occasionally hit its intended target, human flesh.

The raid lasted just five minutes, but the town was badly hit. At least seventeen homes had been destroyed. They were fully ablaze when they emerged from the bridge. Karl sulked on the way home because his beloved records had been broken. He knew he would never be able to replace them during the war.

Helmut started singing Frederick's song. Eventually the others joined in. They strolled down the country lane in two rows, singing as loud as they could.

Chapter Fourteen

It wasn't until morning that Fritz started to worry. His aunt was not yet home. She had been in the village last night playing cards at a friend's house. She said after cards she was going to come home. After all, she never stayed away. Not *his* aunt. She was always fussing over him. If he was late he would be in trouble. She always waited up for him.

Fritz had lived with his aunt for the last seven years. His mother died of tuberculosis when he was seven. His father was a soldier and was killed two years ago when Germany invaded Poland. She was all he had. He tried telling himself that she would be fine, but his stomach was twisted in a tight knot. By noon he set of for the village. On his way, Grandpa Gunthrie and Frederick stopped him.

"Ah, Fritz, come with us. We're having roast pork for dinner." Grandpa forced a smile, jiggling his fat stomach up and down.

"No, thanks. I have to go to the village and look for..." He paused. Frederick's eyes started to well up and he was looking very serious. Fritz could tell something was wrong. "My aunt." He croaked softly chocking on the words.

Frederick never said anything. The tears of pain he was feeling for his best friend told Fritz what he was dreading. Frederick opened his arms to embrace his friend. Grandpa removed his hat out of respect and looked down to the ground. Fritz started to weep.

"Are you sure? She may just be missing." Fritz cried, trying to convince himself.

"Sorry Fritz. The Tommies killed her and her friends last night. The Tommies are now bombing civilian homes." Grandpa Gunthrie gently patted Fritz on the back. "We made double sure son. She never stood a chance. The house had its own shelter under the stairs, but it took a direct hit. If it's any consolation, it would have been instant. She wouldn't have felt anything."

Fritz hugged his friend tight. "I've lost all my family now," he wept.

"Come on son, come home with us. We'll collect your things later," Grandpa said.

"My things? I can stay at my aunt's house."

"Just for a while, son. You can stay in Frederick's room. I will put a spare bed in there for you."

*

The funeral was a solemn affair. There were too many people dying during the war to have a proper service. Her remains were put in a wooden casket and buried in the village graveyard. Eva brought some flowers. She went up into the hills and dug up some edelweiss flowers and planted them next to the wooden head stone. Fritz's aunt had worked at the bakers and rented her small cottage. Gunthrie knew it wouldn't be possible for Fritz to continue living there. If he were discovered living alone he would be taken into care. Gunthrie liked the boy and felt sorry for him so he filed adoption papers himself. It would take several months for them to go through. In the meantime, Fritz could live at the farmhouse with him and Frederick.

Wurzburg social services where not happy with the condition of Gunthrie's farmhouse. It was dirty and full of cobwebs. But the inspector agreed that Fritz was with someone that cared about him and it was obvious Grandpa and Frederick treated him as family. Grandpa Gunthrie knew that the care homes where packed with children. The last thing they needed was another teenage boy to look after. He was given the adoption papers in less than a week. With so many children losing parents, they did everything they could to speed up the process. Outside of wartime, Gunthrie would never have been approved.

Chapter Fifteen

Two days later the Pirates met in the barn cellar. They started to sing and bring a smile to Fritz's face. He appreciated their kindness, but memories of his aunt returned in the unlikeliest of times and places. They learned that it was a squadron of British Lancaster bombers that had bombed the town the night his aunt was killed. Grandpa Gunthrie walked down the steps carrying a box with a cloth over the top of it.

"You got food, Grandpa?" Helmut asked excitedly. The others rolled their eyes.

"Is that all you think about, Helmut?" Eva asked crossly.

"Nope I think about girls too and what I would like to do with them." He sniggered.

"Eww. That is disgusting. It's clear that God made man before he made a woman," she replied.

"Why? Is it because we have more brains?" Helmut grinned.

"No, he made all the mistakes first on the prototype then he made the perfect human." She smiled, stood on her toes, and posed, flashing her eyelids as if she was a model. The boys all groaned as if in pain.

Grandpa passed the box to Karl and stood back, resting his hands on his round belly. Karl lifted off the cover and looked inside. A huge grin ran across his face. His hand dug in and pulled out a record collection. He started reading the labels out loud. "Benny Goodman, Irvin Berlin, Ella Fitzgerald, Glenn Millar. This is brand new; it's just been released. How did you?" He gasped and looked at Grandpa. A tear ran down Karl's face. He put his arms around Grandpa Gunthrie. "But how did you get these?"

Grandpa Gunthrie cleared his throat and turned away to wipe his eyes. "Ask no questions and I shall tell no lies." He grinned. "Now put one on the gramophone and play it as loud as you like. The Hitler Youth won't hear it down here."

"That's just where you're wrong." A voice bellowed from the top of the steps. It was Luis; he started climbing down the steps. The panic stricken teens went silent. "I knew it was your records at the dance. I noticed how upset you got when the Colonel broke them. Eva I followed you here. You lot are Edelweiss Pirates and the ones that have been vandalizing the town and the Colonel's home, no doubt."

Eva stepped forward and opened her mouth to speak. Luis held his hand up in front of her face.

"Save your breath Eva. You've gone too far. I have to report this. You will all be arrested and taken to a work camp, if you're lucky. If you're unlucky, a concentration camp or even shot." Luis snarled.

"Oh yeah?" Grandpa Gunthrie growled.

"Oh yeah. And you're no better old man; we know you've been dealing in black market goods. Your time is up, too. These records are illegal, and you have just adopted someone. Already you're breaking the law." Luis faced off at Grandpa. He pulled out his dagger and waved it at him. Gunthrie put his hand inside his coat and pulled out a luger. German officers used the German made revolver, but if you were Grandpa Gunthrie you could get your hands on anything.

"Put that knife down. Frederick tie him up. I will have to think of a way to dispose of his body." Grandpa ordered. A gasp went around the room. Frederick did as he was told. He felt uneasy with his grandfather's statement.

"Grandpa. he's my brother." Eva pleaded.

"You heard him. He was going to turn you in and everyone else here. We can't let him go," he told her abruptly and pushed the luger against Luis's chest.

Frederick fetched some rope and tied Luis to a support beam. He couldn't look Luis in the eye. Karl walked over to Luis and struck him in the face. Luis groaned in pain. A small trickle of blood ran down from his lip. Karl faced him with his arms folded. He was the tallest of the Pirates and easily as tall as Luis.

"So, Luis. Your sister wants us to spare you, her darling big brother, but you wouldn't spare her or her friends? We grew up together. We're all German. Our enemy is the British and the Yanks, not each other. Remember those bastards killed Fritz's aunt. What kind of race will we be if we can't have a choice of music, dance, or how long I can wear my hair? You've showed us you have no heart or mercy and yet your sister has it for you. How does that make you feel?" Karl's voice was precise and calm.

"Eva is weak. We're all weak. Our enemy is not just the Tommies and Yanks, but the Jews. This is a holy war." Luis spoke like he was making a speech.

"Okay, shoot him, Grandpa." Karl smiled, using his index finger to make circular motions by his temple. "He's brain washed; there's no hope."

"Is it such a crime, Luis?" Eva begged her brother. She took out a handkerchief and wiped the small blood spot from her brother's lip, where Karl had struck him. "Luis what are we to do with you?"

The cellar fell silent. All eyes looked at Luis. It was uncomfortable for him. He was torn with the love of his sister and the love and pride he felt for his country. Grandpa Gunthrie made the first move.

He walked over to Luis and untied him. Luis massaged his wrists.

"Your sister asked you a question, young man. What's it's gonna be? Are you going to have her sent to a concentration camp for having her own mind, along with her friends?" Grandpa asked.

"Not forgetting you, Grandpa," Fritz went on. "I didn't see any of the Hitler Youth families offer to take me in. Luis, Grandpa Gunthrie has adopted me. He is kind and has given me a home. Do you want to send him away too? Is this the dream of the fatherland? Are we so bad, what's our crime? We played a few records that our current government does not like. Our old government didn't mind it and the next one might not. Oh of course our other crime, we never joined the Hitler Youth who go around in large gangs hitting girls like your sister. If you guys are so tough, pick a one on one fight with Frederick." He snarled. "But no, you are the big Luis, big Hitler Youth man. You threw the toys and children's clothing of German people out onto the street just because they use a different church to us."

Luis felt guilty. He eventually spoke with tears in his eyes and a croak in his voice. "So you will let me go? Even though I may report all of you?"

"Yes. I'm not about to start shooting teenage German boys and these kids are not going to hurt you. They just want to be left alone to sing, dance, and have fun. They're not interested in marching and learning how to shoot a Jew," Grandpa told him. He kept his true feelings hidden. If Luis wanted to leave now, he probably would still shoot him.

Luis sighed and sat down on a bail of hay. "Why are you all so nice? You guys actually trust me? I could be lying to you and could turn you in."

Eva smiled. "Luis, if you love me just half as much as I love you, you'll just carry on with your Hitler Youth and leave us alone. You won't tell anyone."

Helmut opened a metal cake tin. He took out a slice of apple Strudel. "Here, eat this. It's a peace offering. My mum made it." Luis gingerly took the slice of strudel.

Karl wound up the gramophone and put on a new record. The unusual group sat tapping their feet, listening to the music and making jokes. Frederick reminded Luis of the great snowball fight they had two years ago. It made them laugh. Luis reminded him of how a snowball went through the baker shop window. As they sat around laughing and eating, Fritz looked at Grandpa and winked. It looked like for now they had gotten away with it.

When the others left, Fritz asked Grandpa, just before going to bed, if he would have let Luis go if he had not promised to keep the secret. "Not on

your life. He was gonna end up as pig food,"
Grandpa Gunthrie barked.

Luis, on the other hand, had no idea how close
to death he had come. Fritz and Frederick settled
into their beds. They quickly adjusted to sleeping in
the same room and becoming stepbrothers. They
decided together to try and clean the farmhouse up.
It was obvious Grandpa Gunthrie wasn't going to
do it.

Chapter Sixteen

Luis was true to his word; he said nothing. Helmut had bumped into him in the corridor at school. Luis looked away and continued down the corridor with his own friends. For now, at least, their secret was safe.

As the war raged on, supplies of fresh food and gas became scarce. With many of the Jewish businesses forced to close, normal supply lines had been interrupted. In peacetime it would be problematic, but in wartime, it was all the harder. Grandpa Gunthrie was making out like a bandit; black market goods cost a lot more money. Grandpa was now also trading food for cigarettes and French wine with some of the German officers. But he too was getting short of supplies. He suspected the German army was storing supplies at an old train station just outside Würzburg. The Germans now patrolled the entire station and the attached farm; trains came and went, but it was impossible to find out information.

At the evening Edelweiss Pirates meeting Grandpa attended, tonight was different. Instead of sitting back and letting the teens plan their acts of sabotage, he needed a favor. As usual, Helmut had brought food. Tonight he had brought German sausages. His mother had cooked them. They would eat them cold with pickled beetroot. Fritz came up with a plan to let down the tires of the entire fleet of Nazi cars and paint the castle walls with the name Edelweiss Pirates.

"Sounds like a good plan guys, but I wonder if you want to do something else tomorrow night. It's gonna take some planning. You have to be stealthy and keep your wits about you," Grandpa Gunthrie announced.

"Sure, what do you have in mind?" Fritz asked. Normally, the teens rejected an adult idea, but Fritz was being extra nice to his new guardian.

Grandpa explained the location of the abandoned train station and the old farm. The farm had a single-track lane going to it and it had a small station that was used to pick up potatoes. With no other houses nearby, it was completely secluded. He said a lot of Nazi trucks went up and down the lane every day but nothing else. Also as far as he knew, no one from the town worked there, so the Nazis were running the entire area. He wanted them to sneak about and see what they could find out. Take a look at the guards who worked there. He figured they could approach them in the town and bribe them for goods. The idea of doing some real spying appealed to all of them and it was agreed they would go tomorrow night. Frederick came up with a plan that they would pose as a group of teens, out on a trek, learning to map read. If they were caught they would all lie about their age and inform the Nazis they were thirteen and preparing for when they were fourteen and could join the Hitler Youth.

The following night couldn't come soon enough for the Pirates. This seemed more like a challenge. Having the army guarding the station rather than the Hitler Youth made it more daring. If they could get some good information for Grandpa it could benefit them all. They had all eaten roast pork this week thanks to Grandpa Gunthrie's last stunt, so they'd do anything to help. And if it meant taking stuff from the Nazis, that was a bonus and made it more exciting.

The four-mile walk took them just over an hour; nightfall had descended to the point where it was difficult to see too much. They crept along a narrow moonlight lane. An owl hooted just above them and made them all jump.

"Stupid bird," Karl moaned.

"It's an owl not a bird," Eva grinned.

"Same thing."

"No, it's not," she argued. "It's a mammal."

"Like hell it is. It lays eggs, so it's a bird."

"So does a platypus and a turtle. They're not birds."

"Will you two shut up?" Frederick hissed. "We have to be quiet. There will be patrols around here."

Helmut made a hoot sound like an owl. They all turned with a scornful look and then saw the funny side. They carried on walking up a wooded hill, giggling over Helmut's hoot.

As they neared the top of the hill, they could sense something was over the other side. Light pollution emitted from something on the other side was making the sky glow with the eerie cold mist. They crept to the top of the hill and peered through the trees. The sounds of the train couplings clinking and the engine hissing and chuffing grew louder as a steam train pulled into the small station. On the other side was something that looked like a large complex of buildings, surrounded by two rows of high wire fences. The atmosphere felt very cold. The entire area seemed out of place in Wurzburg. Whether it fear or the cold, she could not be sure, but a shiver went up Eva's spine.

A blast of icy wind whistled along the valley and Frederick shivered, thrusting his hands deep inside his coat pockets to keep warm. The buildings were made of wood and seemed to have been slapped together in a hurry, using whatever was at hand.

A truck had arrived and there were people in stripped clothing unloading it, passing boxes from hand to hand. This was a secret world. A world that wanted to keep its distance from the nearby town of Würzburg. An armed guard walked past. He took out a cigarette and a worker flinched. It reminded Frederick of a dog he had once seen at the train station. Its owner had repeatedly beat it and kicked it. The poor dog cowered with fear, just like this worker had. Then it came clear to all of them watching why, because the workers were wearing the Star of David sewn onto their uniforms. These were Jews.

"That must be where they store the supplies, in those huge sheds," Frederick whispered.

"Your grandpa will never get anything out of there. It's got armed guards everywhere. Look, even look-out towers on each corner with spot lamps," Helmut murmured. Frederick looked up and observed two guards in each tower. One held his rifle ready. An eerie foggy mist curled around the base of the towers.

"It looks like a prison," Fritz interrupted. They all gazed and agreed it was a prison. Armed guards patrolled the perimeters with German shepherds on leashes. More lights where turned on, lighting up the platform. The Pirates crept down the hill a little closer to get a better look. They were well concealed in the clump of trees on the steep embankment.

"We need to get a closer look," Frederick whispered.

More searchlights around the compound had been activated long before, turning the area into a dazzling collision of black and white. The gates, the barbed wire, the guards with their guns—all could have been seen a mile away, but for the hill that surrounded it. The lights were throwing out vivid shadows, shapes, and ponds of darkness that might offer a hiding place to anyone brave enough to get close.

The doors on the freight cars where opened. Men, women, and children poured out and were forced to stand in lines. Their steaming breath covered their faces. They stood in groups, huddled but not touching, fingers tightly curled in pockets. They shifted nervously from side to side, the lifting of one foot, then to the other. Their boots and shoes made a crunching sound on the frozen ground. No one spoke. The cold had numbed them and the Pirates into silence. The Pirates looked on. It was a truly unbelievable sight.

Men and boys over twelve were made to stand on one side, women and children over six on another. The elderly, infants, and children under six where made to walk into the fenced complex. Many of the old struggled with the walk. Young children screamed as they were literally torn from their mothers' screaming arms.

What followed was the most stomach-churning sight the Pirates had ever witnessed. A mother's infant was taken from her, crying. The mother instinctively fought back and tried to take back her child. A Nazi officer intervened as she fought with a solider. The officer took the infant, threw it on the concrete platform, and stamped on the screaming child's head several times. The babies' skull was crushed. Its mother collapsed to her knees in hysterics. He then pulled out his revolver and shot the woman in the head. A mysterious silence surrounded the entire area. Everything stopped. The hum of chatter from over five thousand Jewish people and the barking guard dogs stopped as if they intuitively knew something so horrific had happened. It was as if Satan himself had risen from the belly of hell. The hiss of the train engine even seemed to get quieter. An eerie cold cloud descended on the area.

The Pirates felt like they were witnessing a bad dream. This could not be happening. Their eyes must be playing tricks on them. Fritz threw up. Eva put her hand on his back and kept him quite while he was throwing up. None of them knew who made the first move or if anyone suggested it, but they all quietly started to creep back up the hill. They crawled on hands and knees; terrified they would make a sound and be discovered. The crawl up the cold embankment seemed to take forever. They were almost too afraid to look behind them to see if they were being followed.

Chapter Seventeen

Once they made it to the summit, they crept down the other side and made the long walk back to Frederick's barn. They branched off into two groups twenty or so feet apart. None of them spoke. Fritz helped them over a wooden gate. Each of them was trembling so much it was hard to get a good grip; their limbs shook uncontrollably. The long hike back seemed a blur. They sat in the barn in silence. Eva wept, followed by Helmut. Despite his toughness, Frederick curled up into a ball and rock back and forth.

Grandpa Gunthrie made his way down the ladder. He was eager to find out what they had found. At first he thought they were playing a trick on him. They never made a sound. He could hear Eva sobbing and assumed maybe they had been fighting with the Hitler Youth again or had fallen out among themselves. Once he took a look at them he knew something was wrong. He scuffled his way towards Frederick and sat next to him. He placed his arm around the boy.

"What happened son; did you get caught?" he asked. When no reply came he wrongly assumed the answer. "So you had to hurt a German patrolman? Don't feel bad, these things happen." Frederick hugged his grandfather, something he had not done for a few years, but tonight he needed a hug.

It was Fritz who eventually spoke. "It's not a storage area. It's a prison. A prison for Jews. They killed a baby and shot its mother." Fritz wept as he spoke. "They just stamped on the baby's head like you would squash a spider."

"Who would kill a baby?" Grandpa said, not wanting to believe the story.

"The Nazis. They killed a baby and shot its mom. They separated the children from the mothers."

"How many was there?" he asked.

"Thousands."

"Nonsense, there can't be that many. Where would thousands of people live? You would need an enormous camp and," he paused. He had heard rumors of such camps. Concentration camps. Rumors that Jewish people were slaughtered, but no one actually believed it. And this was just a few miles away. Surely someone would know about it. "Did you all see this?"

A few heads nodded. No one made eye contact; they just stared at the floor, not really focusing on anything. Grandpa left and returned a little later with some mugs and a large metal pitcher full of hot chocolate.

"You guys are in a state of shock, get this down ya. I remember when Frederick shot his first rabbit when he was seven or eight. Shook him up a bit. But he got over it," he said, passing out the mugs and pouring the hot chocolate.

"This was no rabbit, Grandpa," Frederick replied in a quite monotone voice.

Grandpa looked at his grandson and carried on. "I know son." He paused; he was searching for the right things to say. "I'm doing my best here, I'm trying to help. Cookies anyone?" No reply came. They stared down, looking at the steaming brown liquid in their mugs. Eva put hers down and walked over to Grandpa. She put her arms around him and hugged him and he gently patted her back.

"What can we do, then?" Fritz frowned. He couldn't understand the man's calm, his refusal to accept the gravity of the situation. He felt events slipping out of his control. "What can we do?"

Grandpa twined his fingers together like ropes. "Well, why don't you drink a little more hot chocolate and tell me once more exactly what happened."

Fritz didn't want to drink more chocolate. He'd had more than enough. It was too sweet, too sickly. And he didn't want to tell Grandpa what happened again either. He realized he didn't want to do anything other than sleep. Although that might be hard, to just lie down in the dark. The entire trauma was catching up with him. No, let the others tell him. He'd done his part, all he could do. He wanted his aunt, to feel her hug him, sniff her scent once more. When would God end this misery, why had God not stopped the war, saved the baby or its mother? It was confusing for anyone to understand, let alone an orphaned teenage boy.

The others, it seemed, were no longer even following what was said. They sat lethargically in their chairs.

"Bastards," Helmut cursed.

"Yeah, Nazi bastards," Karl cussed. The atmosphere changed from sorrow to anger. Everything was discussed from contacting newspapers to planting a bomb and even mounting a rescue mission. Grandpa let them vent but became the voice of reason. To go to the newspapers would probably mean a reprisal from the Gestapo and the SS. The SS had a reputation of torturing anyone, including women and children. It would almost certainly mean death. A rescue mission was hopeless; the place was packed with over one hundred armed guards and patrol. All well trained German solders. Bombs, if they could even obtain one and plant them, most likely would hurt more Jewish people than the Nazis.

Helmut eventually stood up and walked over to the cookie tin. It seemed that he, at least, hadn't lost his appetite.

*

It was hard for them all to sleep that night. Strangely, Frederick was thinking about Grandpa Gunthrie. He was impressed the way he took care of him and his friends earlier tonight. Despite him being a petty criminal, he had recently impressed Frederick. Taking in Fritz after his aunt was killed was a gesture he had been surprised at as well.

Since his father's death, his grandpa has been providing food and paying the bills. The small farm had never provided enough income to support a family, so Grandpa Gunthrie has always found other means to make ends meet. Those means where always grey areas, but that was Grandpa Gunthrie. It was in troubled times like these that made you appreciate loved ones more.

March 2012, Stroudsburg Pennsylvania United States

"So you were a tough fighter, Grandpa?" Austin smiled, examining his own knuckles after he had hit Scott McCamant earlier at lunch.

"It was a different world, Austin. I lived on a small farm and often had to fend for myself. I wasn't a trouble maker or bully, but if I had to I could get myself out of trouble." He grinned. "Now we had better get you into your PJs and ready for bed. I had better spend a little time with your sister, too."

"Will you continue tomorrow, Grandpa?" Austin asked, following his grandfather out to the kitchen. "I need to know what you did about the Jewish camp and if Luis reported you. Did Grandpa Gunthrie get arrested?"

"Well he would be your great, great grandfather."

"Shush, Samantha is asleep. I was just coming to get you two. And they say women gossip," hissed Austin's grandmother. She beckoned them both to the dinning table. "I've already made the hot chocolate and you have to try the cupcakes Samantha made." Her head shook slightly from side to side as she spoke. Austin was not sure what was wrong with her. He knew it had got worse from the last time he saw her.

"Probably poison all of us if Samantha made them," Austin grinned.

His grandfather laughed. "Now, now come on, none of that. Tomorrow, tell your sister how nice they were."

*

Austin woke early the next morning. He could hear his grandfather cough downstairs as he made coffee. From the sound of running water came from his grandparents' bathroom as he crept down the stairs barefoot in his PJs, he guessed that his grandmother was taking a shower.

"We're gonna write it on the walls, Hitler can drink our piss," Austin sang as he entered the kitchen. His grandfather turned and smiled.

"Well, that's not exactly how it went, Austin, but a good try. But don't let your grandmother hear you singing that. And the word I used in the song was 'They can drink out pee.' We were a little more polite back in the 1940s."

Austin sat on a stool and watched his grandfather making waffles. "Can you tell me more of the story?" He beamed.

His grandfather nodded. "I will, but it wasn't a good time, Austin. I'm telling you these things because you asked and it's part of our history. It was a terrible time. The sights we witnessed that night affected us all for a long while," Grandpa

Frederick told him. "I moved away after the war; I had had enough of Germany."

"So you just up and left Grandpa?"

"Life has no remote get up and change it yourself," he said sitting down next to Austin and continued.

Chapter Eighteen

Wurzburg Germany 1942

It was difficult for the Pirates at school the following day. Everything was normal. Some younger boys got shouted at for running down corridors. Some girls were told off for wearing a skirt almost to the knee. They still had homework to do, games, math, so everything was pretty much normal. Yet just a few miles away horrific atrocities were being carried out. Many of the under twelve-year-olds and women that arrived at the camp had already been killed. They were told to strip naked and go into a large cellar for a communal shower to ensure it got rid of lice. Once in the cellar they were all gassed, clinging to each other for support and praying for help with their dying breath. Help failed to come from God.

To make matters worse for the Pirates, that day at school they were forced to watch a Nazi propaganda film on how the Jews were subhuman, avaricious, unrefined, greedy, shifty, and menacing. Most were Jews defined physically by their swarthiness, hunched-back hooknose, baldhead, oversize feet, and paunch belly. After seeing films like this and hearing the same thing over and over, many actually believed it.

The movie also said the Jews were thieves and they hated Germany. It also pointed out that in March 1933 throughout the world the Jewish people declared a boycott of German goods. Germany was like much of the world, in a recession. The new German Chancellor, Adolf Hitler, was incensed that such an act would spiral Germany into a depression, so he fought back and fought back far worse than anyone could have imagined. He said he would rid Europe of all Jewish people. Propaganda lessons were taught in all German schools albeit there was some truth about the boycott of German goods, the rest was just lies and hatred. The German young minds absorbed the information like a sponge absorbs water.

After lunch, Gretchen and Eva were walking to math class. Gretchen was talking about a solider who gave her the eye this morning as she walked to school. Gretchen stuck out her chest. She mimicked herself sticking her chest out and swung her hips from side to side. Eva roared with laughter. She was still laughing when they rounded the corner.

Coming towards them was Karl. He smiled and looked down at the ground. Eva immediately felt guilty for laughing and started to cry. Gretchen tried to comfort her. Eva couldn't tell her why she was crying. The picture of the mother and the baby came back and hit her between the eyes like she had been struck over the head. The people were not like the Jews they had seen in the propaganda film this morning. These were real German people just with a different religion. It was bewildering for adolescent minds to comprehend what was actually happening in their country.

Chapter Nineteen

Six-year-old Zelda played templehupfen, or hopscotch as it is known in English speaking countries, on the sidewalk outside her school. Earlier in the day some older girls had marked out the squares and numbers in white chalk. Despite the light rain, she could still see the numbers. She threw a pebble and hopped from one square to another. After twenty or so minutes she grew bored. The last teacher had left for home ten minutes ago. No one would offer her a lift home or even walk with her because of the yellow star sewn to her coat. The word "Jew' was written on it. No one would offer a Jew help, as it was wrong to help them. You would be seen as a Jew-lover and could expect your home broken into and defaced and even get beaten by the Gestapo or the Hitler Youth.

Eventually, after looking down the street for her mother countless times, she decided she would walk the two-mile trip home. It was raining harder now and the wind was getting stronger. She blinked as the wet wind lashed her face. She could see her home. The Star of David that had been painted in white paint was still on the door, but it looked different today.

Zelda tried the door and called out to her mother. It was locked. A wooden beam was nailed across the door. She noticed the windows were also boarded up, so she crept around the back of the cottage. She screamed when she noticed Golly, the family's black Labrador, lying dead at the back step. He had a small blood covered mark in his head. Zelda started to cry for her mom. This later turned into a scream as she noticed some of Golly's blood on her hand. After a few minutes she banged and kicked on the back door. It was locked and boarded up, and her bedroom window was the same.

The neighbors refused to open the door to her, although Mrs. Overfast had heard the young girl pleading for help. Rather than help, Mrs. Overfast turned up her radiogram and carried on cleaning her dishes. Zelda was now wet through, cold, scared, and upset. The only option was to go back to school. It was getting dark, and she was getting more frightened by the minute. Unfortunately, she took a wrong turn. Because of the blackouts, all street lights were turned off, so the town's position would be invisible from British aircraft on bombing raids. With no streetlights, or lighting from any homes, she got hopelessly lost. Eventually she cried herself to sleep under a tree beside a country lane.

*

Frederick waited at the train station the next morning at seven. He went there three days a week to meet Hans. Hans Huebener was a sixteen-year-old waiter who worked in the dining car on the train that traveled from Munich to Frankfurt via Wurzburg. The train would stop for fifteen minutes to fill the steam engine's tank with water, plus food supplies and newspapers would be picked up and dropped off.

Hans walked to the back of the train to meet Frederick. For just over a year they had been meeting. They swapped goods for Grandpa Gunthrie. Hans often spoke of his dislike for the Nazis. Usually, Frederick agreed with him.

"Hans have you heard of a group of guys called the Edelweiss Pirates?" Frederick asked casually. Hans ignored him and sucked on his cigarette. "There was an attack here in Wurzburg this week by them. I heard there are groups of them all over Germany."

Han's studied Frederick. It was a bold question, but considering Frederick was bartering black market goods, Hans thought he could trust him. "We've heard of them and we heard about the attack on a Colonel's house." He grinned.

"*We* heard?" Frederick grinned. In a flash Hans clasped his hand around Frederick throat and squeezed.

"This is no laughing matter. A fifteen-year-old member was hung last week in Berlin. I never meant *we*." He snarled.

"Yes you did. We have to trust each other. Now let me go before I split your nose open."

Han's released his grip on Frederick and put Frederick's collar straight. He quickly scanned the area and smiled at Frederick. "You know who they are?"

"Yeah, you just nearly got your nose broken and split open by one."

Hans threw down his cigarette and shook Frederick's hand with both hands. He gave Frederick a hug. "That was a good job you guys did. But I was telling the truth about the guy in Berlin. He had been held in prison for nearly a year and has just been hung. We're getting under the skin of the Nazi bastards. Do you know they're killing the Jewish people? Even kids, women, rabbis. They don't care. Now, I'm no Jew lover, but that kind of crap just ain't right."

Hans picked up his cigarette and relit it. "I had two SS officers in my dining car a few weeks ago. They were laughing and boasting how they could kill two Jews with one bullet by making them stand back to back with their heads together. I nearly threw scalding hot tea over them," Hans snarled indignantly.

"Bastards. That must have been hard for you to hold back," Frederick stated.

"Na, I gave them some pilchard sandwiches for free. I made them myself and personally donated the sauce." He laughed.

Frederick cringed and felt himself wanting to throw up. "Hans, eewww. That's disgusting." He frowned.

"And what about the two Jewish guys whose last seconds on Earth had to stand back to back with their heads touching each other."

"Yeah, they deserved the special sauce and more." Frederick agreed. He gave a half smile but it still made him feel nauseous.

"Next week I'll bring you some leaflets. Distribute them around. They have all the facts about what's really happening in the war and the atrocities our soldiers are carrying out on the Poles, the Frogs, and even our own people. You get your guys to put them up everywhere, but don't get caught or you'll dangle from a rope. And you never got them from me." The whistle on the train blew. Hans and Frederick shook hands and agreed to meet as usual in a few days. "Oh and what did you mean, the guy who's about to split your nose open? Think you could take me tough guy?"

Frederick laughed. "With my eyes closed and an arm tied behind my back."

It was a comfort for Frederick knowing that there were others across Germany who felt the same way he and his friends did. Although he still felt ill when he thought about the sandwich Hans had made for the SS officers.

Chapter Twenty

Luis and Eva were walking to school next morning. Eva found it hard to keep up with Luis. He marched with great strides like he was trying to catch a train, while she walked two steps to his one to keep up. He paused and walked towards the tree, looking at something.

"What do we have here?" he asked as he bent down and shook the tiny bundle with his hand. Zelda woke up and started to cry. She was shivering and blue from the cold. "Oh you poor little mite what are you doing out here? You're soaked through. Eva help me. I found a little girl."

Eva brushed the hair away from the girls face and smiled at her. Simultaneously both Luis and Eva noticed the yellow star on her coat. Luis immediately stood back.

"Oh she's a Jew," he said, as if he had seen something disgusting.

"No, Luis. She's a little girl who is freezing cold and no doubt hungry." She picked up Zelda and hugged her.

"What are you doing, Eva? Have you lost your mind?" He gasped.

"No, have you? What do you suggest? We just throw her back to die of the cold?"

"You can't take her home Eva. You'll put our entire family at risk. I've tried to forget about you and your friends, the Edelweiss Pirates. But not this; you can't help Jews. Eva, do you hear me?"

Eva ignored him and started to walk home with Zelda.

"Okay, be a hero, but don't risk my life. Take her to your barn. I'll cover for you at school. But Eva, if you get caught, I knew nothing about her, okay?" Luis demanded. Eva ignored him; she had already decided to take the girl to the barn. Grandpa would know what to do.

The Pirates gathered just outside the school gates talking. Helmut was eating a large sausage. They noticed Luis was coming alone. He would never speak to them normally, and they were surprised when he made his way over to them.

"Ah seen the light, Luis? Come to join us?" Fritz teased. Luis squared up to Fritz and glared at him. "Okay, it was just a joke," Fritz croaked.

Frederick moved forward. "He's my stepbrother now, so back off or visit the dentist," Frederick ordered.

"Eva is at your barn. She is helping a Jew! For her sake, pass the kid onto the social services. If Eva gets caught with her she'll be sent away and you lot too, no doubt," Luis barked. He turned and snarled at Fritz. "If my sister gets hurt over this, I'll blame you." He poked Fritz in the chest with his finger.

Frederick pushed Luis away. "You want to try your luck?" Fredrick asked. "Just you and me, without your army of toy soldiers," he added.

"Anytime, Frederick. I would rip off your head and crap down your neck." Luis pulled out his dagger. Frederick walked forward. The Hitler Youth were given a dagger complete with swastika. It was part of their uniform and, as such, they could wear it to school.

Luis studied Frederick. He had witnessed the red haired boy fight a few years ago, when he took on a boy three years his senior and severely beat him. Luis was taller and older, but Frederick had a reputation of a good fighter with a wild temper.

"If you guys care about Eva, please talk some sense into her." He slipped his dagger back into the metal sheaf on his belt and marched into school.

"I thought as much," Frederick grinned. "Well, looks like we have to miss school and help Eva."

Without even discussing it, Karl, Helmut, Fritz, and Frederick walked off towards the barn. Missing school wasn't a problem for them. It was only a matter of time before they would all have to stop going anyway. Hitler Youth leaders had started to go through school registrations. Once they found out the Pirates were all fourteen and not members of the Hitler Youth, they would be forced to join or face detention camp for youths.

Grandpa was walking towards the barn with two large kettles of hot water. Eva had removed the girl's wet clothing and was bathing her. She asked Grandpa to wash and dry her clothing. When the boys arrived they started to help. Helmut ripped the yellow Star of David off Zelda's coats. "She won't be needing that".

Zelda sat silently in the tin bathtub while Eva washed her hair. Zelda had so far not spoken. Her lonely night spent under a tree wet, cold, and hungry had taken a toll on her. Eva was enjoying acting as mother. Taking care of the little girl took her mind off the terrible scene she had witnessed a few nights before. Fritz passed a towel to Eva and knelt down at the bathtub. He used his little finger to gently brush some soap away from Zelda's eye. She looked at him and smiled.

"I'm Fritz. I hate getting soap in my eyes; it stings. We don't want that, do we?" he asked Zelda in a soft voice.

"Mummy will be sad when she finds out Golly is dead. Why was he still at the back door? He should be in heaven," Zelda asked.

Fritz stroked the side of her face with the tip of his finger. "Who's Golly? And you haven't told us your name yet, either. Do we need to call your

Mummy?" He asked. Eva watched Fritz. She admired how well he communicated with Zelda.

"Golly is our dog. I got his blood on my hands. His head was bleeding." She paused and looked at her hands. "Will he go to heaven?"

"Yes, if Golly was a good dog he will go to heaven. What's your name?" Fritz asked.

"Zelda Koffler. I'm six. How old are you?"

"How old do you think?" Helmut asked. "Seven, eight?" He grinned at Fritz who turned around and gave a glare.

"He is older than seven, silly." Zelda giggled.

'Well little Zelda, you *are* a brave girl for six. I'm Fritz and I'm fourteen and that is Helmut. He's also fourteen, although he looks like he's forty."

"Is she your girlfriend?"

Fritz glanced at Eva, who quickly looked away as he blushed. "Zelda, do you know where you live? Do you go to Würzburg Junior School?"

It didn't take Fritz too long to discover her full name and where she went to school. He left Zelda with Eva, while he and Frederick went to the junior school to find out about her parents.

The school was the same one they attended when they were younger. It appeared much smaller inside than they remembered. Fritz asked the receptionist if they had a girl called Zelda Koffler. The receptionist sighed and became agitated instantly.

"I told the Gestapo everything this morning. Don't they communicate with the Hitler Youth?" she asked.

"We're not Hitler Youth," Fritz snapped. "Did she come here and where does she live?"

The receptionist was annoyed by his tone. "Of course she is. Or was, a pupil here. She lived on Ottosrabe just along from the old well." She looked suspiciously at the two boys. "If you're not Hitler Youth, then who are you and why do you want to know?"

Frederick grabbed Fritz by the arm. It was time to go.

She stood and asked again. "I asked a question. The Gestapo will be back. Who shall I say was asking about the *Jewish* girl?" she quizzed, making the word Jewish seem like a curse word.

"Em. We're helping the Hitler Youth. We're joining when we are fourteen next year," Frederick stuttered. They started making their retreat.

"I need your names," she stated.

"I should Cuckoo." Frederick grinned. This was something he picked up from his grandfather.

"Your names," she demanded.

"I'm Sam and he's Diego." Fritz smirked.

She started to write it down and cursed to herself for getting taken by the boys.

The boys ignored her yelling at them and walked out. They walked towards Ottosrabe Street.

They found the house boarded up. At the back of the house they found the dead dog, Golly, just like Zelda had explained.

"He's been shot," Frederick said, examining the dog.

A voice from the other side of the fence made them both jump. "The Gestapo shot him yesterday. He became vicious when they took the Kofflers away. Jews they were." A middle-aged lady said, looking over the back yard fence. "They've been back already once today. Cheeky lot thought I had the little girl. They went right through my house looking for her. What would I be doing with a Jew?"

"The Gestapo took away Mr. and Mrs. Koffler away?" Fritz asked.

"Yes. Who are you with? You look like school boys.," she asked.

"We're Hitler Youth. We came straight from school to help the Gestapo try and find the girl," Frederick lied. The receptionist had seemed suspicious so he expected the neighbor might as well.

"Can I have your names?" she questioned, taking a pen.

Frederick stuck out his chest and shouted at the woman. "We're Hitler Youth, woman. We have to find a Jew. This was the last place she was seen, so you could be in serious trouble. It is not me we're looking for. No wonder this war is taking us so long to win with idiots like you. Heil Hitler." He stamped and saluted. Fritz was shocked but pleased with Frederick's reply. Fritz followed him outside, concealing his smirk. Back on the road walking back to the barn Frederick laughed.

"There, that was better than, what was it, Sam and Diego? Where did that come from?"

"I dunno, but I thought it was funny." He laughed.

When they got back to the barn, they explained everything to the rest of the Pirates. They spent the rest of the day entertaining Zelda, singing, and playing games. They enjoyed the company of a little girl. She had innocence about her, which reminded them of when they were that age before the war started. They still had no plan what they were going to do with her. Frederick taught her his song he wrote. Zelda thought it was hilarious, especially the part about drinking pee.

"Where would she sleep?" Helmut asked.

Grandpa Gunthrie, without thinking, said for a few days she could stay in the barn. The idea was ridiculed. They weren't going to make a six-year-old girl, who had probably just become an orphan, sleep in the barn.

"She can sleep in our room," Fritz explained, "I can sleep with Frederick and she can have my bed." He got a strange look from Frederick. "Head-to toe.

Just make sure you wash your smelly feet." He laughed.

"I'll have a thousand kids living here before the war is over," Grandpa joked.

Eva became Zelda's short-term mother. She wouldn't be going to school for a few days. Instead, she would come over and look after Zelda. She secretly liked the idea of looking after Zelda. After living in the shoes of a near perfect big brother and having mostly boys as best friends, looking after a little girl made a pleasant change. For a few days it seemed to be working out. Grandpa Gunthrie was concerned he had heard that the Gestapo were stepping up the search for Zelda. The Pirates ignored it. They knew he was usually over dramatic.

Luis told Eva she was crazy for quitting school and that the Gestapo wouldn't rest until they found the Jewish girl. Eva scolded him, telling him that she was called Zelda, not Jewish girl. As normal, they got into a heated argument. Luis stomped up the stairs and slammed his bedroom door. Little did Eva know that he was right. The Gestapo had in fact ordered a house-to-house search for the girl.

The Gestapo, with help from the local police, had orders to straighten up the town. The attacks by the Edelweiss Pirates had been tolerated for long enough. The attack on the Colonel's home and his car and the graffiti on the walls around the town with anti-Nazi messages were outrageous.

But the attack on the Hitler Youth camp not only put two boys in hospital, but also prevented the weekend training sessions. This was viewed as high treason and the finger was pointed directly at the Pirates. The school receptionist also reported that two boys were posing as Hitler Youth and asking about Zelda. They strongly believed that the Edelweiss Pirates had the girl in hiding. The Gestapo interviewed her and were not amused with the names she gave them, Sam and Diego.

Chapter Twenty-One

Luis was at an after-school Hitler Youth meeting when he heard the news. For the first time a Gestapo officer addressed them. They, the Hitler Youth, police, and Gestapo, were going to organize house-to-house searches. If that didn't work, all teenagers who weren't enrolled in the Hitler Youth would be brought in for questioning by the Gestapo.

When the meeting was over, Luis ran to the barn and burst through the double doors, quickly climbing down the ladder. Eva was showing Zelda how to dance. The boys sat around listening to the music. When Luis made his entrance, they sat up in shock.

"Luis, you scared us," Eva shouted. Luis ignored her and took the arm off the gramophone. He turned and faced them and told them what was happening. It took a little time to sink in, but eventually they treated it seriously.

"You have to hand her in and promise me you will cut out this Edelweiss Pirate nonsense," Luis ordered. "If not, eventually they'll catch all of you, they'll no doubt suspect me as well, and you'll all get shot."

"What? Then have the Nazis shoot her or stamp on her head?" Eva screamed. Grandpa took Zelda outside to feed the chickens. He didn't think she needed to hear this.

Frederick tried to calm Eva down. It was clear she wouldn't hand over Zelda to the Nazis. For an hour they argued, going around and around. Several times Frederick and Luis came close to fighting. Eventually Grandpa came back without Zelda.

"I put her to bed. I have a plan and it means sacrifices. If not, we could all get shot, and that includes you, young man," Grandpa said looking directly at Luis.

"Me? No way. I have nothing to do with this," Luis protested.

Frederick stood and faced him. "You know about Zelda, and you know we're the Edelweiss Pirates of Würzburg. You're one of us. I could get you an Edelweiss pin, if you want." Frederick grinned.

Luis grabbed Frederick by his collar and pulled back his fist.

"I dare you," Frederick snarled, his eyes staring deeply into Luis's. "I'll shove that swastika armband down your throat."

"Boys, boys, come on, that won't help. This is really serious. We've poked an alligator up the nose with a popsicle stick. Deep down, we knew something like this could happen and now it has.

We have to be one step ahead. Tomorrow, you four boys join the Hitler Youth," Grandpa ordered.

"Yeah, and maybe we'll get pink snow, too!" Karl laughed. "Look, a flying pig!"

Grandpa turned and scowled at Karl. "You will, or you'll end up getting us all shot. Eva, we have to get Zelda out of Germany. Let's face it, she's Jewish and the Nazis aren't playing around. You saw that for yourself the other night. I have a cousin in Switzerland. She'll look after Zelda."

"How are you going to get her through all the road blocks and over the border?" Luis quizzed. "It's too dangerous. You'll get caught, tortured, and give us all away."

"Fly her out," Helmut said.

"Have you let the food get to your brain? How do we do that?" Fritz asked.

Helmut had not thought of that. The others looked around at each other, trying to come up with an answer.

"I think if you guys join the Hitler Youth, it'll throw them off your scent. That includes you, Eva. But you can't fly her out. You have to turn her over to the Gestapo," Luis said.

"Never. I would rather get shot," Eva protested with her arms folded.

"We just need to steal a plane form the Hitler Youth Luftwaffe Air Corps Division," Helmut argued. The others said nothing. They sat in deep thought. It could work, and it was obvious that Eva wasn't going to turn Zelda over.

"There is a Focke-Wulf Fw 56 training aircraft there. I sat in it. It has no need for a key; you just jump in and press start. It's a single seated plane, but Zelda could sit on the pilot's lap," Luis explained.

They started to plan the escape, but came up with a few snags. How would they get into the base? And they needed a pilot who could be persuaded to put his life at risk, steal a plane, and fly to Switzerland with a wanted Jewish girl. Frederick solved the problem of getting onto the base.

"Who can just drive onto the base in his fancy car without being stopped?" he asked. He paced around the barn with his arms behind his back. He was enjoying his moment and what he thought was an ingenious idea.

"Colonel Manfred Von Furz, no one would stop him. Only problem is, why on earth would he want to fly her to Switzerland?" Fritz asked.

"We don't actually need the Colonel. We just need his car and his uniform. We have our own Colonel." They all looked at him puzzled.

"Helmut, remember when we were at the bath house in the steam room together?"

"Err, yeah," Helmut replied unsure where Frederick was going with it. Karl and Fritz grinned at Helmut. "What about it? Nothing happened. Take that look off your face Karl, Fritz or I'll bash you," Helmut growled, his round fat face turning red.

Fredrick saw the joke, shook his head, and grinned. "You remember when someone came in stripped down and sweating and you thought it was Grandpa?"

"Yeah it was the Colonel. I started asking about the pork thinking it was Grandpa Gunthrie coming back in."

"I look nothing like that great, fat, pompous ass," Grandpa objected.

"You looked just like him naked," Helmut replied.

"Eewww, stop it. What a ghastly thought," Fritz laughed.

Frederick went on to explain. "In his uniform and hat, driving his car at night, you would look identical. We would just need to stick on a fake moustache. We can break in and steal a uniform, tie him up, and steal his car. Grandpa, you could drive into the airport without being stopped. We could hide Zelda in the trunk."

"Great plan, Frederick. Just one small problem. He can't fly an aircraft." Luis laughed. "What, do you suppose we kidnap a pilot and have Zelda hold a gun on him? You guys are so dumb. It's no wonder you've nearly been caught."

Frederick looked deflated. He wouldn't admit it, but Luis was right. Who was he trying to kid? They needed to think of something and fast. Time was running out.

Chapter Twenty-Two

The following day the four boys signed up to join the Hitler Youth. When they were asked why they had not joined up yet, they made the excuse that they knew they had to join up when aged fourteen, but did not think it meant their actual birthday and they wanted to join up as a group now that they were all fourteen. Eva joined the League of German girls. Gretchen, who was already a member, was delighted her friend joined up. She was given a uniform and, because they knew each other, Gretchen was assigned to show her the ropes.

A week later they were to pledge an allegiance and they all had to learn the pledge. "I promise to do my duty in love and loyalty to the Fuhrer and our flag." The boys did not actually hate it as they thought they might. They enjoyed the games, tug of war, target practice, and map reading. It was the propaganda that followed. They had to learn the Hitler Youth prayer. Frederick had to control himself. He wanted to laugh when he heard Luis say the prayer while they all stood and bowed their heads. Luis spoke as if he was saying the Lord's Prayer.

"Adolf Hitler, you are our great Fuhrer. Thy name makes the enemy tremble. Thy Third Reich comes. Thy will alone is law upon the earth. Let us hear daily thy voice and order us by thy leadership, for we will obey to the end and even with our lives. We praise thee! Hail Hitler! Fuhrer, my Fuhrer, give me by God. Protect and preserve my life for long. You saved Germany in time of need. I thank you for my daily bread. Be with me for a long time, do not leave me, Fuhrer, my Fuhrer, my faith, my light. Heil to my Fuhrer!" Luis said. When it was over, the others all shouted, "Heil to my Fuhrer!"

As the meeting came to a close, Luis spoke to Karl, Helmut, Fritz, and Frederick alone.

"Well done guys. I saw you were enjoying yourself at the target practice. Frederick you are no doubt hard; you could join the boxing team," Luis smiled. "I know Eva will have a good time with Gretchen tonight. Now you can put this silly nonsense of the Edelweiss Pirates behind you and be part of our great county. We will defeat the British Tommies. Adolf Hitler will salute our troops from the balcony of Buckingham Palace. Their Queen will prepare his dinner."

"Luis. I want the same, but I don't want to be told what music I can dance to or kill my friends just because they choose a different religion to me. That's the problem with the Nazis," Fritz sighed.

"Or sterilize my brother just because he was blinded in an accident. How the hell is that hereditary? You bastards took his soul away, you--" Frederick put his hand over Karl's mouth and pulled him back. Karl was losing his temper. Luis gave a tight lip smile and nodded.

"I'm sorry that happened to your brother. That was wrong. He should never have been part of the sterilization program."

"Maybe there should be no such program," Helmut cursed. "Julius Caesar, Napoleon, and Joan of Arc all suffered with epilepsy. You Nazis would want to sterilize them too."

"You guys are still naive. Give it time and you will see the Fuhrer is right. Goodnight, Heil Hitler." Luis stamped. He swiftly turned and marched away.

Karl pulled away from Frederick. "Should have let me smack him one." Karl grunted. "I could take Luis."

"Yes, I know, but we don't want any trouble until we can get Zelda away and safe."

"I could've taken him." Karl said again. His friends smiled and nodded at him. They knew Luis would easily get the better of him, but Karl was their friend and if it made him feel good, then so be it.

On the walk home they started to laugh about the night's events. They all agreed the Hitler Youth prayer was pretty lame. They waited at the barn for

Eva to arrive. When she turned up in her Hitler Youth uniform they took great delight in teasing her about it. She was wearing a black skirt and white shirt with black scarf tie and a toggle. She had the Hitler Youth diamond badge with swastika on her top pocket. She remarked they looked just as stupid and at least she did not have to wear a red armband with a swastika.

She made a fuss of Zelda. Grandpa brought in some hot sausages. He passed them around a plate with two each, though he gave Helmut four. He knew Helmut would be hungry as usual.

"The police came here today," Grandpa announced. "Luckily, Zelda was asleep. They poked around in the barn and said they would be back. They never found the trap door, but if they come back with dogs we're sunk."

"Yes, Luis told me they are going to use dogs. They have some of Zelda's clothing from her cottage. Those dogs are clever. We're gonna have to move her," Eva said, looking anxious.

"She's right, Grandpa. Maybe we could keep some meat down here. If the dogs sniff their way here, we can tell the Gestapo they picked up on the meat scent," Frederick belched.

Air raid sirens momentarily hushed the conversation. They all agreed they were glad to be living just outside the town center. Fritz looked hurt. They never stopped to think about what had just happened to his aunt. Anti aircraft 'Ack Ack' fire could be heard as German guns shot up at the British Lancaster bombers. The group ran outside to take a look. The massive German spotlights searched the dark skies for the British bombers delivering their payload of death and severe destruction.

The drone from the enemy aircraft was deafening. The night sky was lit up with flashes, bangs, trails of anti-aircraft fire, and the spot lamps.

"Pretty." Zelda smiled pointing her tiny finger up into the sky. Eva picked her up and hugged her. "Pretty, look at that." She smiled again, still pointing up into the sky. It made them all smile to see an innocent child laugh even in the face of a bombing raid.

"We got one of the bastards," Frederick shouted, punching the air so hard he could have made a bruise.

"Frederick. Language, Zelda is right here," Eva scolded. They watched as one of the Lancasters started to slowly drop, its right wing bellowing sparks and flames. They watched as the plane descended in their direction. As it plummeted down, a trail of flames lit up the sky. The thundering shockwaves made the ground vibrate as the British bombs exploded, hitting their intended target in Würzburg. The sky's summit light up in orange plumes as the bombs erupted into skin blistering flames. The huge explosions could be heard a few seconds later as sound waves tried in vain to catch light speed.

"Maybe they'll bomb the school," Helmut grinned.

"Oh yeah, well maybe they'll bomb the bakery or butcher's shop. What would you do then, Helmut?" Karl laughed.

Helmut thought for a moment. "Damn Tommies, clear off back to England." He growled, giving the aircraft flying overhead the finger, much to the amusement of the others.

Chapter Twenty-Three

The British Lancaster crash landed two miles away from the farmhouse. Two of the crew were killed in the air by the anti-aircraft fire. During the emergency crash landing into the woods, the front gunner was killed. Another R.A.F airman was killed as the glass tail turret was smashed when the plane started to spin out of control, hitting a large Oak tree. Finally it came to rest and erupted into a ball of flames.

Fred Weaver, the pilot, looked across at his co-pilot. A large oak branch had speared him. Fred felt for a pulse and felt sick to his stomach when he felt nothing. He kicked away some of the broken glass from the cockpit and jumped clear from the plane. He tried in vain to open the hatch, but the twisted burning aircraft kept its contents sealed tight.

Another explosion forced Fred to cower and retreat, covering his face from the intense heat. As much as he tried, he could not get into the plane to check for survivors. The flaming wreck defended its prey and was not giving up. Exhausted and suffering from cuts and some burns to his hands, he fell to his knees and prayed for help.

*

The German High Command received news that a British bomber was shot down. They urgently needed to know if the crew either parachuted or made a crash-landing. Immediately, a platoon of troops was sent to the area. The local Gestapo was ordered to temporarily suspend the search for Zelda and join in the search for any R.A.F airmen that may have jumped or crash-landed. Catching prisoners was a huge moral boost for German troops and something they wanted to capitalize on.

Fred made his move. Using a pocket compass he decided to head south. If his calculations were correct, he was about two hundred and fifty miles north of the Swiss border. If he could get to Switzerland, a neutral country, he could return to Great Britain. He thought if he traveled at night and slept by day he could cover twenty miles a night and would reach Switzerland in about two weeks. He would have to steal food on the way. It wasn't going to be easy by any means, and being alone and having no weapons with him made it all the harder. But he remembered a speech that British Prime Minister, Winston Churchill, had given a few weeks ago at a London school. Fred remembered reading it in the newspaper and someone had stuck it up on the R.A.F barracks wall.

"Never give in. Never give in. Never, never, never, never in nothing, great or small, large or

petty, never give in, except to convictions of honor and good sense. Never yield to force. Never yield to the apparently overwhelming might of the enemy."

This gave Fred the will to go on, the will to get back to his country to see his son and daughter, and ultimately to get back in an aircraft to defeat his country's enemies. Despite the odds being stacked against him, he set off south. He kept off the roads and followed along on the inside of hedgerows. Every time he heard a car coming, he would duck down and hide. A truck carrying troops raced along the lane on the look out for the aircraft.

Once the army located the plane, they swarmed in with searchlights and dogs. The Gestapo also joined in the search. First reports from the scene said they thought the crew was killed, but after only finding the remains of six of the crew and the pilot's seat empty and broken glass and blood just outside, did they start to search for the pilot.

Fred made his way to the river Main. He cleaned up the cuts on his legs and soothed his burnt hands. He drank the water. It was not pleasant tasting, but when you're thirsty like Fred was, it tasted like champagne. It took the smell of the burning Lancaster away from his throat. He walked along the riverbank's edge for a few hundred yards, keeping his boots in the water. He hoped it would throw off any scent to tracker dogs. He slipped on a moss covered rock and was swept down stream before getting his footing and making it back to dry land.

Finally, he cut back inland and started heading south again. He knew the Germans would be searching for him, so he zigzagged his route. When clouds covered the moon, he was in total darkness. His matches where wet, so he had nothing that would illuminate his compass. It was a helpless situation for the airman staggering around in total darkness, wet, cold, tired, and hungry. He was making slow progress and decided to find shelter before dawn broke. He could make out a small farmyard. It had a small stone built farmhouse, a barn, and a stone outhouse.

Slipping through the darkness, he pulled open the barn door slowly, hoping, no praying, that the hinges wouldn't squeal. A small sound, anything, could give away his presence and cost him his freedom, or worse, his life.

The cold darkness of the empty barn welcomed him. He inhaled the air. "Hmmm," he said to himself. "The wonderful smell of hay!" There was nothing like it in the world! It smelt as good there as it did in England. As his eyes adjusted to the dusky black interior of the barn, he could just make out a rickety ladder to the hayloft. It seemed like the perfect place to stay for the night. The ladder creaked as he gingerly climbed. On reaching the summit, he flopped onto the prickly hay. It was warm and dry and that was all that mattered. A small cloud of golden dust puffed around him. He breathed in the sweet aroma of the dried grass.

He lay back and closed his eyes. He really needed a cigarette. His thoughts changed to food, a warm beer, and then his family. He smiled as he thought about his children. Those thoughts quickly vanished and a tight knot formed in his stomach when he thought about his crew. He hoped that they were all unconscious when the Lancaster burst into flames. The thought of his friends burning alive in pain sickened him. No, he told himself, they were dead or unconscious, for he had heard no screaming.

"Am I actually in Germany? Maybe we drifted and I'm in Switzerland," he told himself. He lifted himself up on one elbow and tried to make out the shapes in the barn. Everything reminded him of a British barn. He had taken his daughter horse riding. The stables looked and smelled very similar.

Chapter Twenty-Four

"Morning, boys. Rise and shine." Grandpa Gunthrie grinned, entering Frederick and Fritz's room. He was still wearing just his long johns and string vest. His vest had gone a grey color because it was washed with his dark clothing. It had also either shrunk or was never big enough. It sat just above his belly button; his large belly forced itself into view. He had a hole in the left knee of his long johns, which matched the holes he had in his socks. As normal he was unshaven. He had more hair around his face than he had on his head.

"Morning, Princess Zelda. How did you sleep?" He smiled, looking at the little girl as she poked her head out from under the covers. She smiled and nodded as she watched Fritz and Frederick climb out of bed.

"Is that bacon I can smell?" Frederick beamed, lifting his head in the air to get a better sniff of the aroma.

"Yes it is, so get lively and get downstairs. We got to get some of the food eaten if the Gestapo is going to come back snooping around."

Fritz scooped up Zelda in a blanket and chased Frederick down the stairs. She was laughing as she bounced up and down. Grandpa limped down the stairs. A huge grin ran across his face when he saw his makeshift family sitting in their PJs, tucking into hot tea, bacon, and toast. He turned on the radio and danced his hips to and fro to the music with a spatula in one hand, frying eggs and his pipe in the other hand.

The sound of the radio woke Fred from his deep sleep. He crawled to the eve of the barn roof and peeked through a hole in the timbers. He was surprised at the sight he could see through the kitchen window below. It made him smile. An elderly overweight man in his underwear was dancing to music while cooking on a stove. He could see some children wearing PJs sitting around the table. Then his stomach screamed at him as he noticed they had food and what looked like hot mugs of tea. Still, it amused him to see the strange family dancing. It brought back memories of his own children.

Fred climbed down from the barn and crept out the door. He went around the back of the barn for a bathroom break and set off across the fields. He planned to find a tight clump of trees where he could hide until it got dark, maybe get his bearings and find some food. He had only gone half a mile and realized he forgot his compass. He cursed at himself. "You bloody fool Fred, forget your head if it wasn't screwed on." He made his way back. All seemed quiet. He sneaked in and started to climb up the ladder when he was discovered.

"Who are you?" Eva asked. She was coming up from the hidden cellar. He could not speak German, so he continued up the ladder, grabbed his compass and started to come back down. "I asked you a question." She crossed her arms. Eva noticed his torn pants and cut on his leg. He was wearing a leather sheepskin bomber jacket. She spotted the wings on his jacket. At first she ignored it. After all, it looked like a Luftwaffe pin without the Swastika. She looked closer. "You're a Tommy," she shouted wide-eyed. She turned to run.

Fred acted fast. He didn't want to hurt the girl but he had to keep her quiet. He caught her and put his hand over her mouth. She kicked and scratched him. Eventually, she bit his hand. She let out a small scream before he held his hand over her mouth again, this time much tighter. He threw her on the ground and landed on top of her. He looked around for something to tie her up with. He could see nothing, so he started to remove his belt to restrain her.

Eva became hysterical. She had heard about the atrocities the Russian Red army had carried out on German women. She thought the worst and thought the British solider was removing his belt to lower his pants. She clentched and managed to get a hand free. She stuck her nails into the back of his hand. The skin on Fred's hand was already sore and swollen from the aircraft fire. "Aghh," he cried. "Hold still girl. I'm not going to bloody hurt you," he cursed. Eva continued to struggle.

The barn door opened and Fritz stepped in. He looked in disbelief when he saw Eva pinned down by a man, her face red and eyes full of tears. Fritz screamed at Fred and dove on him. Fred and Fritz wrestled and rolled across the floor. Eva climbed to her feet and ran towards the house screaming for Frederick. The struggle inside continued. Both Fred and Fritz fell down the trap door to the cellar, both of them hitting their heads as they fell. It momentarily stunned Fred. Fritz was not fazed; he started to pummel Fred, calling him every curse word he could think of.

Fred shook his head and tried to focus. He caught hold of Fritz's hands. He noticed Fritz had a deep gash on his forehead that was oozing blood. "Hold bloody still, boy. You're hurt." Fred groaned. He used his weight advantage and pushed Fritz on his back. He now had Fritz held down. "Please stop fighting, you're hurt. You'll make it worse," Fred pleaded. Fritz continued to struggle and curse and spat at his attacker.

Frederick jumped down the last few steps of the cellar and landed a perfectly aimed kick to the side of Fred's head. The forceful blow knocked Fred off Fritz and knocked him out. For good measure, Frederick gave the unconscious man a couple more kicks in his side. Grandpa Gunthrie climbed down puffing and panting. He was carrying his luger; he pointed it at Fred and looked around the cellar to take everything in. Frederick was already attending to Fritz's head wound. He placed his hand over the gash to prevent further blood loss. Fritz was drenched in blood.

Eva came down and screamed when she saw the condition Fritz was in. She looked at the airman. She gasped. "Did you shoot him?"

"No, Frederick dealt with him," Grandpa said as he went through the airman's pockets.

"Shoot him, Grandpa. Look what he did to Fritz and he tried to..." She paused as if it was too horrid to say. "He tried to! You know... me."

Frederick got up and kicked the airman again. "Filthy Tommy Pig, she's only fourteen." He spat.

Grandpa passed his gun to Frederick. "If he wakes up and tries to move, shoot him. I'm going to take care of Fritz." Both he and Eva helped Fritz to stand and took him back to the cottage. Karl and Helmut arrived, both wearing their Hitler Youth uniforms. They were concerned when they saw the condition of Fritz and then went down to take a look at the British airman. They were impressed when they saw Frederick holding a gun to him.

"Is he dead?" Helmut asked.

"No, I kicked him, but if he moves I'll shoot him. Did you hear what he was gonna do to Eva?"

"Yeah and we saw what he did to Fritz." Karl walked over to him and kicked Fred in the side again and again. "That's for bombing Fritz's aunt and that's for hurting Fritz."

Fred coughed and became conscious. He slithered on the floor in pain, eventually lifting himself up on one elbow. He was clearly in some discomfort.

"I'm gonna get Luis. He'll go bananas when he hears what this dirty pig was going to do to Eva," Helmut said, although he really just wanted to get out of the cellar. Seeing Karl kick the man who already looked half dead didn't fit well with him. He ran down the farm lane and headed on the same road he knew Luis would be on. He didn't have to go far. Luis was on his way to school.

"Luis, we've got a load of credibility now. We'll be the pride of the Hitler Youth." He beamed. "You have to come over to the barn."

"I'll be late for school. Why, what has happened? What have you idiots gone and done now? Maybe you have kidnapped Adolf Hitler? Or agreed to use Grandpa's field as a landing strip so we can get invaded by the Tommie's?" Luis sarcastically asked.

"A Tommy airman is at the barn. He attacked Eva and tried to, um, you know, do that to her. And he kicked the stuffing out of Fritz and split his head open. Frederick got the better of him though." Helmut beamed.

"Is Eva all right?" he asked as he set off sprinting towards the barn. Helmut wasn't an athlete; he walked back instead.

Luis raced towards the farm and went into the farmhouse. He put his arms around Eva and hugged her. She was surprised by his affection. He kissed her head and looked at her in the eyes. "Are you all right Eva? Do you want me to get mum for you?"

"I'm fine thanks, Luis. He didn't have a chance to do anything. Fritz fought him off me." She sniffed. Luis looked at Fritz. His head was now bandaged and he looked better, although his shirt was covered in blood. Luis gave Fritz a tight-lipped smile and nodded his thanks.

"For a small guy, you did well to take on a Tommy." Luis smiled. Eva walked over to Fritz and held his hand. He was clearly enjoying the show of affection from Eva.

They made their way back down to the cellar. Eva followed them down. Fred was sitting up. When he saw more arrive in Hitler Youth uniforms he decided to just give himself up. He was still hungry and now his body ached all over. Helmut finally made it back and joined them. He was the only one who could speak English, so was given the job of translation. He stuck out his chest and paced up and down. "So Englishman. What's your name?" he asked with authority.

"Fredrick Archibold Weaver. Squadron Leader. Serial number 165221975," Fred glumly replied.

"And what was your mission?" Helmut asked.

"Fredrick Archibold Weaver. Squadron Leader. Serial number 165221975." Fred replied.

Helmut wasn't expecting the same reply. "I never asked that again."

"Fredrick Archibold Weaver. Squadron Leader. Serial number 165221975," Fred replied smugly. "That's all you're getting out of me mate."

"I see, you're sticking to the Geneva Convention then?" Helmut asked.

"Yes."

"Please Fredrick Archibold Weaver, Mr. Squadron Leader. Where in the Geneva convention does it say you can rape fourteen year-old-girls?" Helmut asked. He repeated what he had asked to the others. Luis smiled and grinned. "Or attack a school boy. Fritz is only fourteen."

Fred tried to stand until he saw Frederick wave the gun. "I would never do such a thing. I have children myself. She was screaming and biting me. I wanted to tie her up and get away. I only came back for my ruddy compass. I never hurt her or him." He pointed at Fritz. "We both fell down that ruddy hole up there. When I saw what he did to his noggin I tried to help him."

Helmut looked puzzled. "What's a noggin?"

"His head." Fred smiled.

Helmut explained what Fred had told him to the others. He asked the Squadron Leader why he had her pinned down and was removing his pants. Again Fred explained that he had just taken his belt off, nothing more. It was just to tie her up so he could get away. He certainly had no intention to remove his pants or any other clothing. They got into a group and discussed what to do next.

Fred smiled at Zelda. "How old are you? I have a daughter who's four. You look a little older." Fred asked. Helmut translated for Zelda, and she grinned and told him six. Helmut repeated the figure to Fred.

"So you're all one big family?" Fred asked.

"No, Frederick and Fritz live here with Grandpa Gunthrie. Zelda is Jewish and we're hiding her from the Nazis," Helmut replied.

"But you're all Nazis aren't you?" Fred asked puzzled, pointing at Helmut's armband. Helmut translated the conversation back to the others.

"You stupid fat fool." Luis cursed. "Why did you have to tell him you were hiding a Jew here? What if he tells the Gestapo that part when we hand him in? We'll all get shot." Luis shouted and cursed again. Helmut bit his lip; he knew he should have left that out.

Grandpa asked everyone to remain calm; name-calling was not going to help. Fred looked up at Eva and said sorry, he was only trying to stop her from shouting. If she thought he had other intentions, she was wrong and he was very sorry for frightening her. Helmut translated, and then Fred apologized to Fritz. He explained he never once hit Fritz. His intention was to just leave, and it was Fritz who attacked him. Although Fritz agreed, he said nothing. He was enjoying the attention he was getting from Eva.

"I'll go to the Colonel and tell him that the Hitler Youth captured the English airman. We may all get accommodated for this," Karl grinned.

"Then what? Tommy here says we're housing a Jew and we all get shot," Grandpa groaned. They all looked at Helmut. He was feeling bad enough already about the slip of the tongue.

"We have to hand her over as well. We can say she's been hiding in the barn," Luis said.

"That won't be happening. They'll send her to the camp," Eva argued. They all went around and around, arguing and not really getting anywhere. Fred asked for a drink of water and Grandpa brought them all down more bacon sandwiches and hot tea.

"I must say, you Krauts eat ruddy well. Our bacon is on ration," Fred grinned as he bit into a bacon sandwich. Helmut laughed and translated. They all laughed when they heard what he said. Helmut explained to him it was here as well, but Grandpa had means and ways to get stuff.

Helmut asked Fred why he referred to them as *Krauts*. Fred didn't know and asked why they called the British *Tommies*. Helmut laughed and never knew the answer to that either.

All this time Frederick said nothing. He was in deep thought, watching the airman, Eva, and Zelda. Eventually, he straightened up in his chair and cleared his throat. He asked Helmut to translate something. "Ask him if he is just the crew or the actual pilot."

"I already told you I am a Squadron Leader. That means I'm a pilot in charge of a squadron," Fred explained.

Frederick nodded when Helmut translated it. Frederick smiled, took a mouthful of tea, and stood up.

"Here's what we'll do. Helmut, translate this to the Tommy while I speak," Frederick began. "We not only hide Zelda in the Colonel's trunk; we also hide the airman in there as well. Ask him if he can fly a Focke-Wulf Fw 56." Before Helmut could ask, Luis stood and shook his head.

"Frederick, I thought it was Fritz who bumped his head. Are you seriously suggesting we let this English pig steal a German plane so he can fly back to Britain and return and drop bombs on us again?" Luis spun his index finger around his temple and laughed.

"Are you forgetting what he tried to do to Eva? You want to trust this piece of dirt with Zelda?" Karl gasped.

"He has explained that. He never tried to do anything to me. He was just trying to restrain me and stop me from screaming. Wouldn't we do the same?" Eva argued. She had picked up on Frederick's plan and, if it meant saving Zelda, she would fight for it. "Imagine if you were in England in a barn and someone was going to scream the place down, wouldn't you want to shut them up too?"

"Eva, he killed my aunt. How would you feel if it was your mum? He's our enemy," Fritz reasoned.

They never got anywhere. As far as Luis was concerned, they should hand him in and Zelda. Grandpa was unsure what to do. He knew they couldn't risk the airman informing the Gestapo about Zelda. He had an idea. It wouldn't be popular, but to him, it was the only logical solution. It took him a while to suggest it.

Grandpa eventually suggested that he shoot the airman. They could say Fritz tried to hold him, a scuffle started, and he had to shoot the Tommy to save his grandson and Fritz. It would mean one less Tommy dropping bombs. They wouldn't have to steal a plane that Germany needed to train its pilots and then maybe the Gestapo would assume they were a model German family, full of Hitler Youth members. They would decorate them and might forget about Zelda and not search the farm.

The idea seemed to have merits, but was still a risk for Zelda and who was going to shoot him? In many ways he was just like them. Zelda had sat down next to him. He took out a notebook and pencil and drew a picture of Mickey Mouse flying an aircraft. She was delighted with it and sat on his lap while he drew her some more pictures. Helmut stood over the airman, stuffing a bacon sandwich in his face. His portly figure stood over Fred as he questioned him with his mouthful. "Can you fly a Focke-Wulf Fw 56?"

Fred thought for a minute. "If it has wings and an engine, I can fly it. I've flown bi-planes, a Wellington Bomber, and of course Lancasters. Why do you ask? Do you want to enlist me in the Luftwaffe?" he joked. Helmut translated it back to the others and added that he didn't feel right killing a guy in cold blood. That would make them just as bad as the Nazis.

"We're Edelweiss Pirates; we don't kill women, children, and prisoners of war," Helmut sighed.

"I'm a Nazi and proud of it. You've all sworn an oath and should be too," Luis barked.

"I lied," Eva grinned.

"I had my fingers crossed, so it doesn't count,." Frederick laughed. "But Helmut is right, we can't shoot a prisoner. He's just like us, fighting for his country." Helmut translated it to Fred.

"We're all in the same boat, following orders, I fight for my country and you fight for yours. The only difference is, your leader is a raving lunatic," Fred grinned. "He's a bloody madman."

Helmut roared with laughter, and the others laughed when he translated it. All except Luis, of course. The conversation went back to flying Zelda to Switzerland to Grandpa's cousin. Helmut informed Fred about the details of the plan. At first he was leery; he found it hard to believe. Was this an evil stunt so they could shoot him trying to steal a plane?

Helmut was eating again and between mouthfuls he and Fred continued to chat. Fred enjoyed talking to him. His own son was fifteen and Helmut and the others reminded him of his son. Helmut loved talking in English, even more so because the others didn't know what he was talking about.

Fred wondered what his son would do if he came across a German pilot. Probably not help him steal a plane and fly home, that's for sure. Helmut explained to Fred everything about the Edelweiss Pirates. It was difficult for anyone to understand them. They were patriotic to their country, they wanted to win the war, yet they hated Nazis and the rules they enforced. They hated being forced to join the Hitler Youth, not being able to play certain music, wear certain clothing, or say anything they felt.

Although he would never admit it, these things bothered Helmut more than seeing the Jewish businesses closed down. He, like many, had blocked out the idea that the Nazis killed them. He was like so many Germans who assumed they had been shipped off to Madagascar, an island just off the African coast, where they could form a new country and build new synagogues.

The camp near Würzburg must've just been a holding camp before the Jewish people were sent off to Madagascar, Luis had told them. He said it was secret because many of the Jews were wealthy and the Nazis didn't want the German people trying to steal from them. The sight of the mother and baby had told a different story. Luis couldn't explain it. Like many German people, when the subject of brutalities was brought up, they tried to ignore it and pretend it wasn't happening. It made them sleep a little easier, if nothing else, but did nothing to help those getting slaughtered right under their noses.

Chapter Twenty-Five

Wednesday morning

The weather had changed for the worse and a drizzle pelted the glass as Frederick lay on the bed in his PJs. He lifted himself up onto one elbow and peered out the window. The rain had brought with it a morning mist that clung to the trees. He had been awake most of the night making a plan. He was still finding it hard to sleep with Fritz sharing his bed. Quite often he'd woken up to find one of Fritz's toes almost shoved up his nose. He was thankful for small mercies that Fritz kept himself clean, probably something his aunt had instilled in him.

Grandpa never said much to Frederick regarding hygiene, but now he was forced to share a room with Fritz and Zelda, Frederick kept himself cleaner than normal. There were some advantages to having a new stepbrother. This morning Fritz had offered to feed the chickens and clean out the cow pen.

Frederick worked out the escape plan in fine detail. The biggest problem they had was Luis. He still refused to go along with it. He couldn't stand by and watch a British airman steal a German aircraft and escape, only to be re-united with his squadron of Lancaster bombers where he could come back and bomb Würzburg again, killing more of their friends and family. Frederick was unsure how to deal with Luis. He had put his hopes in Eva and her powers of persuasion. If the plan were to succeed it would have to happen tomorrow night, just after the Hitler Youth meeting. The Gestapo was searching everywhere. It would be a miracle if they didn't come back to the barn to search again. Having Fritz and Frederick being members of the Hitler Youth took the farm off the radar but only temporarily.

Frederick tried to get dressed. He looked around for a clean pair of socks. He knew he had a clean pair out.

"That damn Fritz has got my clean socks on." He cursed. He looked in the laundry basket, through the dirty socks trying to find a matching pair. When he found a couple of pairs he held them up to his nose, trying to find a pair that smelled the least. He was annoyed that Fritz had taken them but enjoyed having him around. He glanced in the mirror, spat on his hand, and tried to push his red hair in place. It didn't want to move, so he left it sticking up in all directions on one side and flat on the other where he had been lying on it.

He wouldn't have time for breakfast before going to the train station to meet Hans and then going on to school. "Yuk school," he said to himself. It was Wednesday, which meant French, math, and science. His heart fluttered with nerves for the briefest moment. He would get nailed because he had not done his homework. Then again, so what? They would just send home a letter and Grandpa would never say anything. Although, he pictured the dirty look he would get off Mr. Brack.

*

Frederick watched a man with the small dog as he waited for the train. The man kicked the dog for no reason. The dog's tail was firmly between its back legs. Frederick could hear the train. It was late, but that wasn't unusual. Since the invasion of Poland, nothing seemed to run on time. When the train pulled in and stopped, he stood back, waiting for Hans. Grandpa had given Frederick two bottles of French wine. He wanted at least a kilo of bacon or a kilo of cheese for the wine. Frederick also carried cigarettes, just in case Hans had any extra items he wanted to barter. He waited patiently for Hans. Eventually Frederick grew impatient and walked down on the tracks. He crept along the other side of the train, out of sight.

He opened the dining car door and climbed up into the carriage. "Hans," he called. At first nothing, then a noise came from the kitchen.

"And you are?" A man in a waiter's uniform asked sternly, looking down his nose at the scruffy red-haired youth.

"Oh...Um I'm Gustav," Frederick lied. "I was looking for Hans." He stuttered and stepped back. The small chink of the wine bottles touching from under Frederick's jacket gave him away.

The waiter smiled. "So, you have something you want to exchange?"

"Err. Yes, sir." He gulped, not knowing if he could trust this man. And where was Hans?

"Not here, wait at the back of the train. I'll come out for a cigarette. What's your favorite food, son?"

"Bacon sir, I love bacon. I eat it by the kilo." Frederick smiled. The waiter gestured with his hand for Frederick to leave. He stood and waited at the back of the train. The waiter surveyed up and down the tracks. When he was positive the coast was clear he climbed down. He limped up the tracks towards Frederick; he looked nervously around again before he pulled out a paper package that was bulging from inside his jacket. He opened it and showed Frederick.

Frederick passed him the two bottles of wine. The waiter paused and read the labels.

"French Chardonnay, very nice."

"Where's Hans today?" Frederick asked.

"That filthy traitor was shot."

Frederick almost dropped the bacon he was so horrified. "What? No. Why did they shoot him?" Frederick stuttered the words, trying to smile.

"He was found with hundreds of sheets of lies about our country, trying to spread the lies. We have our fellow countrymen getting killed by the Tommies and he was helping their cause. If it wasn't for losing my leg I'd be standing along side them." He tapped a bottle against his left leg; it made a clonk sound. "I lost it in a battle in Czechoslovakia. Good riddance to Hans. I've lost many friends and family. I'm sure even you have?"

"Yes, sir, my father," Frederick glumly replied. The train whistle went. The waiter turned and limped back up the tracks to his dinning carriage.

"I'll see you again. Yes?" he probed.

"Yeah," Frederick shouted back, although he was not sure that he would actually meet the guy again. He would talk to his grandfather about the situation and get his advice.

Frederick noticed a man in an overcoat and trilby standing at a door on the platform smoking a cigarette, shielding its glowing tip between cupped hands. Apart from looking up at Frederick as he smoked, the man barely moved at all and seemed oblivious to the cold. Frederick climbed up onto the platform and increased his pace, keeping a watchful eye on the man.

At the last moment the man dropped his cigarette to the ground where it joined a pile of used butts. He carefully ground it out before slipping away into the shadows. Frederick felt very uneasy about him. *Was he Gestapo?* He anxiously asked himself. He thought about Hans and felt guilty. *Was he bringing the papers to me to distribute when he got caught?* It didn't bear thinking of. Frederick knew this was no longer a game. Although he wasn't elected leader of the Würzburg Edelweiss Pirates, the others looked up to him. For everyone's sake he now had to take extra precautions and trust no strangers. They would have to suspect everyone if they were to survive the war. Joining the Hitler Youth had been an ingenious idea of Grandpa's.

As Frederick rounded the corner of the platform, he noticed the man with the dog again. He was complaining to the platform attendant about the train being late. The attendant told him there was a war on and if he didn't like it, he should write to the Fuhrer himself and complain. The attendant walked off. Frederick sniggered.

"Something funny *boy*?" The man sneered. Frederick never normally caused conflict, but the man in the hat, the death of Hans, and the sight of this man beating his dog troubled him.

"Yes, I thought it funny what you were told. Let's face it, a cruel bully like you probably can't write, let alone have the guts to write to the Fuhrer." Frederick gestured at the poor dog. He faced off at the man, hoping he would say something back, looking for any excuse for him to take his pent up frustration out on the man.

The man did nothing. He could see the determination in the boy's eyes. He may have only looked fourteen, maybe fifteen, but the red headed boy's eyes were bulging and his top lip curled up. "Yes, well there, is a war on. I must get going. Good day." He gulped and yanked the dog's leash as he scurried away.

Chapter Twenty-Six

Grandpa took his horse and buggy into the town just after five that night. He dropped off two sacks under the old main bridge just below Fortress Marienberg. Fred and Zelda stayed in the barn cellar. Fred was both excited and terrified. He had to trust the Pirates who, in his eyes, had already betrayed their country, and he had to fly a German plane he hadn't even heard of, let alone seen. He was driven forward by the words of Winston Churchill. *Never, never, never give up.* It kept his spirits up; he wasn't about to give up now.

Helmut, Karl, Fritz, and Frederick went to the Hitler Youth hall. Fritz told a convincing story to everyone that the gash on his forehead was the result of being attacked by the Edelweiss Pirates. He boasted how he bravely fought three of them off, but eventually their larger numbers got the better of him. Frederick managed to hold back his grin. He whispered to Fritz that he should take up acting.

Eva met her best friend Gretchen and attended the League of German Girls. Eva hated it. Tonight, Fraulein Crouse was going to teach the girls how to iron a man's shirt correctly. Eva rolled her eyes and yawned. Fraulein Crouse looked down over her glasses at Eva and stuck her hands on her hips, picking up her body action.

"Ah, Eva, it looks like you already know how to do this?" Fraulein questioned.

"Yes I do, Fraulein." Eva sighed. Her mind was elsewhere. She hated the League of German Girls and although she was going to miss Zelda, she had already promised herself that once little Zelda was safely away and the British Pilot was gone, she would quit.

"Good, then you can demonstrate. Come on, now get up here and show us how to iron a man's shirt. And I want it done properly. Creases must be parallel; the collar must be perfect."

"No, I'm good. I'm sure you're a better instructor than me. You have had so many *more* years of practice," Eva sneered with a curled lip.

"That was not a request, young lady, it was an order. Get up here and show us how it's done."

Eva yawned and dragged herself up from her seat. Slowly she slumped forward. She turned back and grinned at Gretchen. Gretchen didn't smile back. She had known Eva since kindergarten and knew she was about to make a scene. Eva took the iron from Fraulein and asked her to step back.

"So girls, when you get married and you get your husband's shirt, this is what you do." She turned to Fraulein. "Fraulein, you can play my husband." Fraulein Crouse nodded in agreement. "So you take the shirt and lay it on the table and you take the iron and pass it to your husband." She passed it to Fraulein. "And you say 'Do it yourself; I'm not your slave. I have enough to do. I'll also have a job, so I won't be ironing anyone's shirt unless it's for my own children."

A few giggles came from some of the girls. Gretchen couldn't hold back her laugh either. Fraulein was furious and slammed the iron down on the table. "How dare you insult the League of German Girls. In all my years, I have never heard such insubordinance."

"What insubordinance? What's that? Don't you mean insubordination?" Eva grinned, clearly enjoying her rebellious act. She started to walk back to her seat with a large grin.

Fraulein was infuriated. "You get back here and iron this shirt," Fraulein shouted. As she did, she made a grab for the iron by the bottom and not the handle. "Aghh. Ouch," she cried quickly, dropping the scolding iron. Eva sensed she had gone far enough and started to leave.

"Get back here you little Schlampe," Fraulein cursed.

"Leck mich am Arsch!" Eva grinned as she made her speedy exit. She felt good about what she had done. She was going to be a modern woman, get a job, and earn her own money. The League of

German Girls aimed to train young girls how to be mothers. The posters of the Mothers Cross everywhere and the fact that girls not much older than Eva wanted to get pregnant so they could increase the Aryan race just annoyed Eva even more. She was blonde, but Fritz had dark hair and big brown eyes. How dare they say he was only part Aryan and that she should consider getting a boyfriend more like Karl just because he was blond with blue eyes. She felt a tinge of guilt for not following along with tonight's plan, but now she could spend a little longer with little Zelda.

Chapter Twenty-Seven

The boys at Hitler Youth were split into teams of fours. They had to take a section of town and knock on doors asking questions about the British airman. If any homeowner seemed suspicious or appeared to be hiding anything, they were to send someone to report back immediately while the others kept watch. Armed with a list of addresses and a pencil, the groups of boys set off. Luis suspiciously eyed Karl, Helmut, Fritz, and Frederick as they marched out. He was still adamant that he would not help the British airman escape.

The boys found the two sacks that Grandpa Gunthrie had left under the bridge. They pulled out the contents of one. Karl and Fritz climbed into dark coveralls. They picked up the other sack and ran towards the Fortress. Helmut and Frederick stayed at each end of the street as lookout. Karl opened two large tins of white paint, threw a brush to Fritz, and grinned as he plunged his paintbrush deep into the white liquid. The two boys worked fast. Karl wrote in huge six-foot letters '**Edelweiss Pirates rule Würzburg**' across the bottom of the Fortress. Fritz was writing a British song that Fred had taught them that all the boys all thought was hilarious.

Hitler has only got one ball
The other is in the Albert Hall
As for Himmler
He's somewhat similar
But Mussolini has none at all

Once they had finished the artwork, it was off with the coveralls and on to phase two of the plan. Frederick would now run back to Hitler Youth HQ. Helmut, Karl, and Fritz headed to the Colonel's home.

*

Eva had made it back to the farm early and just as well. Grandpa Gunthrie was getting nervous and had second thoughts.

"Grandpa, you haven't shaved yet. Come on, hurry. The Colonel is always clean shaven." Eva fused. She tried to calm him down and get him ready.

"I can't do it. I'm not as young as you lot. I'll have a heart attack before the night's over. If I get caught, what will happen to Fredrick? And now I have Fritz to care for as well." He puffed.

"Grandpa, if you get caught we'll all get shot. You won't have to worry about them anymore."

"You're cold hearted Eva. Can't see what young Fritz sees in you," Grandpa sighed.

Eva's ears pricked up. "Why, what did he say about me?" She blushed.

"Wouldn't you like to know? Are you sure we can pull this off? What about that headstrong brother of yours?" He asked.

Zelda came into the kitchen chewing a strip of bacon. In her other hand she had a glass of soda. "I cleaned my teeth, Eva." She smiled.

Eva looked at her, puzzled. "How?"

"Grandpa says bacon and soda is good for my teeth." For a brief moment Grandpa and Eva looked at each other before bursting out laughing.

"Princess Zelda, I said baking soda is good for your teeth, not bacon and soda." He laughed.

*

Frederick had run down Main Street. He took his final corner and slowed down. A black Maybach SW38 car was parked. It wasn't the car that caught Frederick's attention; it was the man standing outside. He was wearing a black trench coat. He stood smoking a cigarette and wearing a black trilby. Frederick recognized him from the train station. Frederick put his head down and carried on walking.

"Emhum." The man coughed. "Err, young man, I need to talk to you."

Frederick didn't have the time. He had to follow through with his plan. "Sorry sir, I don't have time. We have an emergency I have to deal with.," Frederick said.

"An emergency? Then I need to know what the problem is."

"I'm sorry sir, it's military business and national security. I can't say," Frederick replied. He was getting nervous. The man took out his card and passed it to Frederick. He glanced down and read it. Commandant Richard Baer of the SS. Frederick froze he felt sick to his stomach. His panic-stricken face was flushed.

"Em, yes sir." Frederick stuttered as his heart raced. *He can't know our plan for tonight*, he told himself. "Then you should come with me, sir. I have some important information." Frederick walked on. He briefly stopped and looked back. "Are you coming, sir?"

The Commandant smiled and followed Frederick. He doubted the boy had anything of national importance but was very interested in Frederick. They entered the Hitler Youth HQ. He ran inside shouting for the Colonel. The Colonel was with another youth leader, Rolf. Both were discussing what they would do if they come across the enemy pilot. Both the Colonel and Rolf eyed the man following.

"Colonel, Colonel." Fredrick panted. "Edelweiss Pirates, we saw them. They've written slogans all across the Fortress and some treacherous rude stuff about the Furher and Himmler, sir."

"Did you get a good look at them? Do you know who they are?" the Colonel asked, jumping to his feet and checking his gun.

"No sir, they ran off. Helmut, Karl and Fritz have gone after them, sir. Oh and this is Commandant Richard Baer of the SS." The words made both the Colonel and Rolf stand at attention.

Commandant Richard Baer saluted. "Well, it sounds like you're busy. I shall be back and we shall speak some more. Go and take care of the Edelweiss Pirates."

Rolf left on his motorcycle, while the Colonel left together with Frederick. Frederick was told to wipe his feet before entering the car and not to touch anything; he didn't want finger marks on his car. The Colonel himself put gloves on to drive.

"So you know that SS commandant?" the Colonel asked.

"No not exactly." Frederick sighed. He was confused about the commandant and what he wanted. But for now he had a plan to follow through to completion.

*

After having a rare shave, Grandpa set off across the fields to the Colonel's cottage. The skies started to fill with dark clouds as dusk begun to settle. Most people would have a problem going cross-country in the dark. Not Grandpa Gunthrie though, because he knew the land better than anyone and was used to being out in the darkest of nights hunting, poaching, or just plain avoiding the police and other landowners.

Helmut, Karl, and Fritz arrived at the Colonel's home. They broke the back door window and gained entry. Fritz and Karl ran upstairs to find some clothing for Grandpa. Helmut headed to the kitchen. He found a large assortment of food and was quite happy sampling the different cakes, cookies, and sausages. Fritz and Karl found what they needed. They started to make the trap. Helmut painted slogans on the outside wall.

Down with the Nazis.

Hitler is a Moron.

Hitler Youth wear Diapers.

Edelweiss Pirates 2 Colonel Manfred Von Furz 0.

Rolf rounded the corner to the fortress. A small crowd had gathered to see the graffiti. The song brought a few smiles to some of the on-lookers, though they tried to look outraged. No one had seen who did it. Some Hitler Youth members had also turned up and were frantically searching for the Pirates.

The Colonel drove a steady twenty-five miles per hour. He didn't want to risk having an accident in his prized possession. He had spent a small fortune having the paintwork repaired after the Pirates branded it. Frederick strained his neck looking out the window. He knew what route the Colonel would take and knew that if he looked across the fields he would be able to see the Colonel's home. It was getting dark. He could hardly make it out, but if the plan was to work, he had to try.

"Colonel. The Pirates! They're at your home painting the walls!" Frederick shouted. The car came to an abrupt halt. Colonel Manfred Von Furz strained his eyes, and he could just about make the outline of his cottage in the distance.

"I can't see anyone. What can you see?" The Colonel asked.

"Look, someone is painting words on your house. Can't you see that?" Frederick replied, pointing and knowing full well that he could not see anything either.

"No."

"You need to eat more carrots, Colonel, or get your eyes tested. Look, someone is there. We can catch them red handed," Frederick said excitedly.

"Yes, I see something. Hold tight," the Colonel lied. He crunched the car into first gear and sped off. Frederick had his fingers crossed that Helmut had actually had time to write something on the Colonel's cottage. If not, his cover would be blown. He also checked behind to ensure the commandant wasn't following.

*

Eva put some extra clothing on Zelda and explained that she was going on an airplane ride with Fred. It would be cold up in the air. It would be dark and noisy too, but Fred would look after her. Zelda was excited. She liked Fred even though she couldn't understand anything that he said to her. But he had a warm smile and trusting blue eyes. She had never been in a plane before and was looking forward to it. Eva had told her that when you look down, people are so small they look like ants.

Fred was studying maps of the airport and Switzerland. He also flipped through a manual they had stolen on the Focke-Wulf Fw 56. It was in German, but he managed to make out the important things. It had a range of 365 miles. He was going to head south to Wagenhausen, Switzerland. He worked it out. The direct flight was about 215 miles. Everything seemed to be working out. Just as he was about to put the map down, he panicked. A tight knot developed in his stomach. The stupid children hadn't planned for that.

"Damn you bloody kids," he cursed. Eva looked up. She couldn't speak English, but she could tell he was perplexed about something.

The map was in miles, but the aircraft manual was in kilometers. He quickly did the calculations, and at first he thought he was going to be short on fuel for about a hundred miles. No, that couldn't be right. It's just over two hundred miles for the entire trip. He worked it out again; it had been sometime since he had been to school and could work out how to divide miles into kilometers. Or was it the other way around? Eventually he breathed a sigh of relief. It worked out to around three hundred and thirty kilometers or two hundred and five miles, and the plane could carry enough fuel to fly three hundred. He would have enough as long as he didn't encounter a very strong head wind.

"It's okay; I take back what I said about you kids." He smiled at Eva. She still had no idea what he said, but he seemed happier now, so she smiled at him. Fred opened his top pocket and took out a creased black & white photo. He passed it to Eva .She studied it and smiled. It was a picture of a small girl and teenage boy.

"Ihre Kinder?" She smiled.

"Yes, my children." He grinned. "My children."

*

Grandpa made his way to the back of the cottage. He couldn't see the Colonel's car, so he kept out of sight. This point was critical to Frederick's plan. No one could get seen. If they were it would mean their cover was blown. They would then have to take drastic action that could result in killing someone. This, above anything else, they wanted to avoid.

Chapter Twenty-Eight

Fritz and Karl put their coveralls on again. They also put a pillowcase over their heads. It had slots cut out for eyes. They taped the cases on each other securely. They couldn't risk them coming off or twisting and being unable to see. They waited inside the house patiently. They heard the sound of the Colonel's car, followed by the thumping of their racing heartbeats. Nerves were on edge. They began to shake, both with fear and excitement.

The Colonel and Frederick climbed out of the car. Its lights illuminated Helmut's handy work.

"Look what the pigs wrote," Frederick said. Deep down he was dying to laugh. The one line, Hitler Youth Wear Diapers, was hilarious, and he would have to congratulate Helmut for that line.

"Shush," whispered the Colonel. "Get behind me." He started creeping towards the house. To Frederick's horror, the Colonel pulled out a pistol from inside his jacket. He forgot that the Colonel would be carrying a gun. Now they had a big problem. Fritz and Karl could get shot. The plan was to wrestle him to the ground, put a sack over his head, and then Karl and Fritz would tie the

Colonel and Frederick up. This would keep Frederick's cover. But a gun blew a hole in that plan. He would have to think of something else and quick.

Slowly, the Colonel crept to his front door. It was left slightly jar. Frederick followed close behind him. He was considering wrestling the gun away himself, but the Colonel was a huge heavy guy, probably had strong hands, and would know Frederick was in on it.

*

At the end of the Richthofen Airfield, a solitary figure climbed up and over the barbed wire fence. His fit body effortlessly made its way over the top. He stopped to get his bearings, re-adjusted the rifle case he had on his back, and crouched down, heading toward the aircraft. The Focke-Wulf was standing just outside an old wooden hanger. As he came out in the open, he lay on his front, took his breath, and started the long agonizing crawl toward the plane. His face was blackened with black boot polish. He was wearing dark coveralls and a black knitted hat to cover his blond hair.

Two Hitler Youth Air division stood guard at the gatepost. They rested against the wooden boom gate and lit a cigarette. As customary, the conversation went from girls, to cars, and back to girls again. The position of standing guard on the gate was the most hated part of the Hitler Youth. It was tedious and freezing cold. It felt more like punishment to the young teens who could come up with a hundred other things they would rather be doing.

*

Grandpa slowly climbed over the gate at the back of the Colonel's cottage. Helmut was peeping around the side of it. He had also noticed the Colonel's gun and was concerned about Fritz and Karl.

The Colonel pushed the door open with his revolver. The door gave a high pitched squeak. He stopped to wipe the perspiration from his brow. Frederick was right behind him, breathing down his neck. He noticed a figure coming from the side. It was Helmut carrying a trashcan. He had removed his boots so he could creep silently. In a swift motion, Frederick took the trashcan and raised it over the Colonel's head. The Colonel's attention was inside his cottage, so he never noticed Frederick dropping it over his head. Frederick let out a scream, as if he had been hit himself.

Frederick pushed the Colonel to the ground and wrestled with the pistol. The initial shock was enough to get the pistol away from his grip. He passed the pistol to one of his hooded friends and fell back on the floor. The Colonel struggled and managed to get the trashcan off his head. His eyes darted around his living room. Frederick sat crossed legged with his hands raised. Two hooded figures wearing black coveralls stood over them, one of them wielding the Colonel's pistol.

"Have you gone raving mad? Do you know who I am?" screamed the Colonel. The temples in his forehead swelled in anger.

"Swinehund, shut up or I will shoot you." Frederick recognized Fritz's voice. Fritz followed up by kicking the Colonel. "We are the Edelweiss Pirates and we will not stop until the Nazis give us back our freedom." Frederick found it hard not to smirk. Fritz was speaking in a deep voice that sounded so fake it was comical.

Karl took a bundle of the Colonel's clothing outside to his car. He met Grandpa Gunthrie and told him all was going to plan. Grandpa sat in the driver's seat and got acquainted with the modern car's controls. Helmut carried on painting slogans on the Colonel's cottage.

"What do you want?" The Colonel challenged.

"Your uniforms. Take them off," Fritz demanded. Slowly, the Colonel and Frederick undressed to their underwear. Karl came back in and watched them. He whispered something to Fritz. Fritz laughed out loud. Frederick was puzzled. The plan was to tie them up and leave, but they seemed to have other plans.

"Your underwear," Fritz ordered the Colonel.

"What?" The Colonel was outraged.

"You heard and you too, Hitler Youth boy," Fritz ordered again. Frederick shook his head. This was not the plan. He glared at Fritz.

"Do it or I'll shoot." The Colonel removed his underwear. Slowly Frederick did the same, glaring at Fritz the entire time. Fritz knew that later he was going to get thumped by Frederick, but for now made the most of it.

Karl came back in and roared with laughter when he saw them standing naked. He picked up a rope and tied Frederick's hands behind his back. He did the same to the Colonel. Fritz was shaking with laughter so much his stomach began to hurt. The more he laughed, the more Frederick got angrier. His eyes were bulging out of his head. Karl then tied the Colonel and Frederick together back to back. For good measure he wrapped the rope around their legs and tied the end to the cast iron stove.

Fritz approached the Colonel. "I need a souvenir from you Colonel. I can turn you Jewish with one snip." He looked down at the Colonel's private parts. "Or your moustache. Which will it be?"

"Neither. You'll have to kill me first." He cursed.

"Well, if you don't give me an option we'll take the moustache and make you Jewish. And maybe your Hitler Youth boy friend can be made Jewish too." Karl chuckled.

"I'm going to kick your teeth in if I ever get hold of you," Frederick screamed.

"Colonel, make it easy on yourself and your friend just relax. You can grow a new moustache. We aren't so horrid that we want to have you bleed to death." Karl pulled out a pair of scissors. "Hold still, you don't want me to slip and drop the scissors. You don't know what they'll snip off if they fall to the floor." In a swift move, Karl cut off the Colonel's handlebar moustache. "There now, that didn't hurt, did it? You can keep that little thing." He grinned at Frederick.

Karl was laughing; he put on a deep voice. "Don't worry, we'll of course close the door so you two can be alone. Besides, it looks like you're cold." He sniggered. They closed the door and left them tied up to the stove. They climbed into the back of the car laughing hysterically.

Chapter Twenty-Nine

"What's so funny?" Grandpa asked as he started the car.

"We made them both strip naked. You should have seen Frederick's face when I gave him the order." Fritz laughed.

"Oh, ha ha." Grandpa laughed. "You know he'll get his own back on you for that."

"Yeah, but until then we can enjoy the moment." Karl roared. Grandpa let out the clutch. The engine roared to life. The back tires spat up stones as it pulled away from the Colonel's cottage.

"Don't worry boy. Someone will find us and we'll have our day. We'll catch them and you will get your chance to kick their teeth in," the Colonel told Frederick.

*

The weather in Würzburg was uncertain tonight, it was bitterly cold, if you sat outside too long you could easily get frostbite. The wind felt like it was cold enough to freeze liquid hydrogen.

The darkened figure had made his way to the aircraft hangar. He kept low and sneaked inside. It was an old hanger from World War I, a dark open space, built from large oak beams, elm wood walls and roof. The old building was full of cobwebs and mice. Inside, he found two small airplanes that had been stripped down and the wreck of an SG38 Glider. He suspected that someone had been seriously hurt when they crash-landed. Another hung from the ceiling. A large red banner flag with the swastika hung from the back wall.

Along the right side was a long workbench full of tools, maps, cans of oil, and what looked like instruments from an aircraft cockpit. Everything was covered with a thin membrane of frost. He settled down at his vantage point, opened his rifle case, and took out a double-barreled shotgun. Now he just needed to sit and wait.

*

Grandpa and the boys swung into the farmyard. Grandpa was enjoying his new toy, though he knew he wouldn't have it for very long. They spilled out and ran into the barn. Eva, Fred, and Zelda were waiting for them. "Everything go okay?" Eva asked.

"Yes although we made a slight change to Frederick's plan." Fritz laughed. Helmut and Karl started to laugh as well. Even Grandpa had a chuckle.

"What change?" Eva asked. "Grandpa go and get changed into the Colonel's uniform." Fritz explained to Eva the change of plan they had made.

"Do you mean poor Frederick is tied up next to the Colonel, naked?" She grinned.

"Yep." Karl laughed.

"He's going to go crazy with you guys," she laughed.

"Yep." Fritz grinned. He was thoroughly enjoying the moment.

Grandpa struggled to squeeze into the Colonel's uniform. He normally kept his own pants up with twine, and he never tucked the front of his shirt in as his belly forced it out. He came back to the barn struggling with the jacket.

"You boys got the wrong uniform. This must be his old uniform he wore when he was younger."

"No Grandpa, that's the right one. Why, are you saying you're fatter than Colonel Manfred Von Furz?" Fritz smiled.

Grandpa grunted and continued to struggle with the jacket. He eventually got it on, but he couldn't do it up.

"Sit down on the couch and lay your head back," Eva ordered. She looked at the moustache they had cut from the Colonel. She applied candle wax to it to hold its handlebar shape. She gently placed the moustache under Grandpa's nose. "Fritz, pass me the candle." She dropped a few drops of hot wax on the moustache. A drop hit his nose.

"Steady on girl, that's hot," Grandpa complained. The others laughed at his moaning.

Eva took a step back and admired her handiwork. Fritz passed Grandpa the helmet. He put it on and stood. The others were amazed at the resemblance.

"You look just like him Grandpa." Fritz smiled.

"Yep, maybe just a little heavier," Karl joked. "Come on we'd better get going. If the Colonel and Frederick get free too quick and raise the alarm, they'll be on the look out for his car before we're done."

They gathered outside. Eva gave Zelda a hug. It was a tearful goodbye for both girls. Fritz made a fuss of Zelda before she left. Fred said his goodbyes to Eva, Fritz, and Karl. He took a moment with Fritz. "Sorry, mate. We got off on the wrong foot. You're a bloody good fighter for a boy." They shook hands and exchanged a smile. Fritz was not sure what he said but it seemed friendly and that was good enough for him.

Helmut was missing. "Where's Helmut? Eva asked.

"He went for a walk," Karl said.

"He's a little nervous." She smiled and passed a cup of milk to Zelda. He came back through the farmyard gates with his hands in his pockets.

"Okay, it's now or never." He forced a smile.

Helmut was going with Grandpa in his Hitler Youth uniform no one would suspect anything. Frederick planned it that way, just in case something went wrong. He could translate anything to Fred.

Fred climbed into the trunk. Zelda got in on top of him. It was a big adventure for her; she was enjoying it. "Heil Hitler." Grandpa saluted Eva, Karl, and Fritz. They all laughed at his attempt to act like the Colonel. Helmut sat in the passenger seat and grinned at Grandpa.

"You *really* look like the Colonel, Grandpa," he beamed.

"This had better work. These pants are killing me," he puffed. They set off towards the Hitler Youth Air Division airport. "My Frederick is a chip off the block. His plan is perfect. We can get little Zelda safely away to Switzerland and that Tommy back to his family."

"So he can come back and bomb the crap out of us." Helmut sighed.

"I liked him. He was okay, showed me how to make rabbit snares out of copper wire. Shame he couldn't speak German though." Grandpa smiled. As they drove down the main street Grandpa noticed a motorcycle was following them. "Maybe I spoke too quick. We're being followed."

Helmut turned to take a look. "Uh oh, it's Rolf. He's a Hitler Youth leader. Keep going. Are you sure he's following us?" Rolf continued to follow them as Grandpa took a few turns off the main street. Eventually he pulled over and he took out his gun.

"Don't let him see your face," Grandpa told Helmut. Rolf stopped his bike and walked up to the driver's window. Grandpa wound it down. "Rolf meet us back at HQ." Grandpa put his foot down and pulled away, leaving Rolf in a cloud of fumes. He seemed confused but didn't for a second suspect anything. He assumed it was the Colonel and Frederick. Grandpa watched him disappear in his side mirror.

They got back on the main road and gave a sigh of relief when they realized they got away with it. It took them just over half an hour to drive to their destination. The guards at the gate were still leaning against the boom gate chatting. They both clapped their hands together trying to keep warm. When they noticed the car headlamps coming they stood to attention. Grandpa drove up to the gate and honked his horn. They immediately opened the barrier. He drove forward a few feet and stopped. Helmut wound down his window.

"Hi guys, the Colonel is going to show me around. I'm thinking of joining the air division," Helmut lied, keeping his face turned away pretending to be looking at his dagger.

"Yes sir," they both said. Grandpa looked across and nodded at them and then drove into the compound. He headed straight for the hanger.

Grandpa pulled up next to the plane. Helmut jumped out and opened the trunk.

"We're here. The guards can't see us from the gatehouse, but we have to be alert just the same," Helmut ordered. Fred looked over the aircraft. He climbed up into the cockpit and turned it on. It was only half full of fuel, and he would have to fuel it fully if he was to make it to Switzerland.

"It needs more gas," Fred told Helmut. They went into the hanger together and found some gas cans. They filled them up from a huge gas tank that was sitting on some blocks just outside. The cans were heavy when full. It made Helmut's arm ache holding it while it filled, so he hooked the can on the tank faucet while it filled. Regrettably when it was nearly full, the weight snapped it off.

"Oops," Helmut stuttered. He quickly put the next can under the gushing gas. "I broke the faucet," he cried to Fred who was coming back with two empty cans.

"We only need another one and we'll have enough. I'll take this one. See if you can plug it with something." Fred grinned, taking a full can.

*

Frederick guessed that enough time had lapsed for Grandpa to get Fred and Zelda to the Richthofen airfield. He used his foot and dragged his pants with his toes closer to himself. "Colonel bend down with me, I think I can reach my dagger."

Frederick managed to get his dagger and cut themselves both free.

"Good work boy." the Colonel nodded. They quickly dressed and made their way on foot to the village. Frederick wanted them both to be seen before the plane took off. He was surprised how quickly the Colonel could walk.

"Shall I run on ahead sir and raise the alarm?" Frederick asked.

"Yes. Get Rolf and if the SS Commandant is there still, let him know what just happened."

Frederick took to his heals and sprinted towards the Hitler Youth HQ.

*

When Fred emptied most of the can's contents into the plane he did a final check and came back to the hanger. Helmut and Grandpa gave up on trying to plug the hole. Helmut was soaked in gas. "Wow, what a waste and a mess. Don't you know there's a war on?" Grandpa joked.

"Yes exactly, there's a war on." A voice came from behind a stack of pallets. A tall slender figure wearing black coveralls and boot polish on his face appeared holding a shotgun. It was Luis. "Put your hands up where I can see them. All of you."

"Now look Luis, this is about the girl, nothing else. If he doesn't take her the Nazis will ship her off to a concentration camp. If she's lucky enough to survive the journey she'll either be used for experiments or killed. Take my word for it," Grandpa protested.

"And you'll be shot for impersonating a German officer," Luis stuttered and started a speech he had learned by heart. "My program for educating youth is hard. Weakness must be hammered away. In my castles of the Teutonic Order a youth will grow up before which the world will tremble. I want a brutal, domineering, fearless, cruel youth. Youth must be all that. It must bear pain. There must be nothing weak and gentle about it. The free, splendid beast of prey must once again flash from its eyes. That is how I will eradicate thousands of years of human domestication. That is how I will create the New Order."

"Luis, that's bull. Wake up and smell the roses and realize what would happen if you report this. They'll shoot us all, including Eva," Helmut argued. "In the end, we're all just people. It doesn't matter where you come from, who you are or what church you go to. Think what they will do to Eva." He hoped to appeal to Luis's better nature, though Helmut was wondering if he actually had a better nature.

"No, they won't shoot you guys or Eva. You can go Helmut. Gunthrie won't speak about you lot. He'll take all the blame himself, won't you Gunthrie?" Luis quizzed.

"Not if they torture me. I'm old, son. They may get me to speak. They will hurt Frederick. Please don't do this. It's for one little girl, that's all."

"No, it's freeing a British bomber pilot. The very same pilot who was bombing our town. And the girl's a Jew. We need to clean our country from this vermin."

"Vermin? *Vermin*? She's a little girl who went to the same school we did when we was her age, Luis. Just because her parents are this religion or that religion or no religion at all, why does she become vermin?" Helmut argued. It made Luis stop and think. He briefly lowered the shotgun. It was long enough for Fred to rush him and grab the barrel.

They fell back against the stack of pallets. The shotgun went off into the ground causing a spark, the leaking fuel whooshing into flames.

"Helmut get out and stay clear, you are soaked in gas," Grandpa ordered, worried that if he got to close he would explode in flames. Grandpa scooped up Zelda and carried her back to the plane. He lifted her into the cockpit and rushed back to help Fred.

Luis and Fred continued to wrestle on the ground dangerously close to the flames. The shotgun went off again. This time it shot through the roof. Grandpa was almost on them when a full can of gas exploded into flames. A plane fuel tank exploded into an enormous ball of fire. Seconds later the whole building was in flames. A third vast explosion caused some of the roof timbers to falls and part of the building collapse. Grandpa retreated. All he could see was flames, which temporarily blinded him. Fred came running out. He was coughing but he seemed unharmed.

Grandpa checked him over, "Is he hurt?" Grandpa asked. Helmut spoke to Fred. He was just shaken and had not been injured.

"Get out of here and quick," Helmut ordered. Fred placed his hand on Helmut's shoulder and nodded goodbye. He shook Grandpa's hand and ran to the plane. They watched as he started it. Fred waved. Zelda sat on his lap she waved at Grandpa. Fred increased the revs on the plane and turned it around. Grandpa and Helmut jumped into the car and waited for him to take off.

*

Frederick rounded the corner towards the Hitler Youth HQ. He was a little concerned that he might have acted too hastily. He noticed the SS Commandant talking to some of the Hitler Youth boys and Rolf. Frederick had to act now or his cover would be blown. He just hoped that the others had followed through with his plan and Fred had managed to take off.

"Heil Commandant and Rolf, we've been attacked and the Colonel has been tied up," Frederick shouted. He found it easier to act like he was in shock because he was extremely nervous. "Commandant help us."

Rolf caught hold of Frederick. "Calm down boy and tell us what has happened," Rolf stated.

"Sir, the Colonel, me, tied up. They had a gun; I think it was the Pirates, sir," Frederick stuttered. The Commandant stepped forward and caught Frederick around the throat. He squeezed and slapped him across the face with his other hand.

"Calm down and start again. Where's the Colonel?" he probed slowly. Frederick gulped; he was pleased he never had to act.

"He's coming. I ran on ahead, sir."

"Where is he coming from?"

"His cottage sir; we got tied up."

The Commandant threw Frederick into his car. "Follow us," he ordered Rolf. The wheels of the commandant's car screeched as he sped off. Frederick gave directions. He looked behind and could see Rolf giving chase on his motorcycle.

"Look sir, the Colonel," Frederick pointed.

"I have eyes boy. Don't speak until you're spoken to," the Commandant barked. They pulled over next to the Colonel. He was sweating and breathing heavy. He sat heavily on the car's running boards. "Are you injured?"

"No sir, it will take more than a few traitorous men to hurt me," the Colonel wheezed.

"Tell me everything that happened," the Commandant demanded. "Every detail."

Frederick climbed out of the car.

"Are you okay Colonel?" Frederick asked still putting on his act.

The Colonel nodded. "Yes, thanks to you, son," The Colonel fought to get his breath back and explained the events. Rolf climbed off his motorcycle. He was staring at the Colonel. Eventually he interrupted him.

"Colonel, what happened to your face? You look different." The Colonel put his hand up to his face and felt where his moustache had once been.

"Swinehund. Damn Pirates cut off my moustache," he screamed. The Commandant couldn't swear on it, but for the briefest second thought he noticed Frederick smirk.

*

Luis was trapped under an oak beam. Once he regained consciousness, he tried in vain to lift it, and all his efforts had no effect on the heavy beam. He stated to cough more violently. Scorching hot flames got closer and closer to him. The roof of the building was ablaze now, the ceiling becoming an intense flaming cloud blistering of heat. Sweltering embers of burning wood rained down all around him. He screamed for help, but the roar of the fire and the aircraft engine drowned any of his cries.

Inside the car Helmut and Grandpa could hear nothing.

A foot-long piece of burning wood fell directly onto Luis. He struggled and managed to flick it off. His hands burnt as he beat out the flames on his clothing. He put every ounce of strength he had into moving the beam and freeing his legs. He screamed in frustration, and then wept for help. Luis's life was flashing before his eyes as if the devil himself danced around him in the burning hellfire.

Fred had turned the plane around. He started to increase the revs on the plane while holding it with the brakes. He looked to either side and something caught his attention. He looked again at the barn. He could just make how someone's hands were waving and pleading for help. He looked away down the runway. All he had to do was release the brake and within a minute he would be up and away, away to freedom, away from Germany and safely to his family.

"Bloody kids," he cursed. He cut the engine pushed the glass roof back and climbed out.

"Something's wrong with the plane," Helmut said. "Fred is getting out." They watched Fred run to the barn.

"Stay here, Helmut. If you go near that fire you'll go off like a firecracker," Grandpa ordered.

Fred ran into the barn, dodging the flames. The roof creaked above him. Fred thought to himself this is what hell must look like. He tried pulling Luis out, but the boy's leg was stuck. He searched around and found a metal pole. He scorched his hands as he picked it up and placed it under the beam and started to lift. It was heavy and not giving way much. He noticed it suddenly got easier and heard a groan behind him. Grandpa was behind him and lifting as well. Once it was high enough Fred held it while Grandpa pulled Luis out from under the beam. Fred growled as he forced himself to hold the weight in he blistering heat. Once Luis was clear he dropped it.

Fred bent down and picked Luis up and ran to the exit with him over his shoulder. Grandpa ran with them. As they got through the door the roof collapsed. Fred carried Luis to the car and laid him on the back seat.

"Colonel, what happened?" one of the guards asked Grandpa. Fred, Grandpa, and Helmut froze for a second. They hadn't noticed the boy approach. The fire alerted him.

"Em, did you guys call the fire station?" Grandpa asked.

"Yes, sir."

"Good job guys. Open the boom gate and keep back or this whole place may blow."

"Who's he?" asked the youth, pointing at Fred in his British Royal Air force uniform.

"Ah well, this is a secret mission. He's our top spy. He's flying to Britain to spy as a British pilot." He turned and looked at Fred. "Well get going man. Take off." He waved Fred away with his hand.

Fred ran back to his plane and climbed in. He started it up again and prepared for take off once more. Grandpa pulled along in the car. He waved at Fred. Fred looked back. He noticed Luis in the back. At first Luis looked away then he slowly raised his hand. He nodded thanks. Fred nodded back.

Grandpa moved the car away and watched as the plane bounced along the grass runway, gaining speed. The small plane roared up into the night sky. Fred had planned to fly as high as he could. He wanted to avoid being sighted by any aircraft. He was even concerned that a British plane would shoot him down.

*

Frederick was first to hear the plane take off but he pretended to ignore it. Rolf shouted the alarm. The Colonel was still explaining to the Commandant what had happened to him and Frederick. They all looked up at the sky. The small aircraft in the moonlight was just visible.

"Why aren't we shooting at it?" the Commandant roared.

"It's one of ours sir," Frederick replied. He felt like jumping up and down and screaming at the top of his lungs. It was really hard for Frederick to control his emotions.

"It's come from the Richthofen Airfield," Rolf suggested.

"Something smells bad here and it's not just your BO, Colonel, but I promise I will get to the bottom of tonight's events," the commandant said.

*

Grandpa and Helmut drove out to the compound. He smiled at the guards at the gate when he drove passed. He dropped off Helmut at the farm and picked up his own clothing. Then he drove the car to the Main River and let it roll down the riverbank into the water with the Colonel's clothing. It disappeared below the water. It frustrated Grandpa to destroy such a beautiful car. He quickly got dressed, cursed when he pulled off the moustache, and made his way home across the fields.

Chapter Thirty

It was an enormous embarrassment for the Colonel. When he found out his car and uniform were used to get onto the air division compound he promised he would not rest until the culprits were found. He was extremely infuriated over the loss of his prized car. It took him just over a year to grow a new full size handlebar moustache again. This hurt him just as much as his beloved car disappearing.

The Gestapo and SS carried out a full investigation. Both the Colonel and Frederick were taken in for an interview. Frederick was terrified the commandant knew something about the escape and was imagining a gravestone with the words *'Frederick Schmidt aged fourteen.'* The Commandant sat across a desk while Frederick was escorted in wearing his Hitler Youth uniform.

Frederick saluted. "Heil Hitler," Frederick stamped.

"Heil Hitler," the Commandant sneered. He tapped his pen on the desk. "Frederick Schmidt, the Colonel has given me a full account and I have heard your version of the story, but there are a few coincidences and I don't believe in coincidences.

Firstly, our paths have crossed before. I noticed you at the train station while you were peddling black market goods, or was that not you?" He watched Frederick's reaction. His eyes burnt into the boy looking for a sign of weakness, anything that might give him away.

Frederick paused he took a deep breath. "Yes, sir, it was me. My father was killed fighting for our country. My grandfather looks after Fritz and me. Grandpa is old and doesn't earn enough to support us, so he barters a few things to make ends meet. It was me, sir. I was swapping wine for bacon. I will ensure it stops immediately. I want to be German officer one day, sir, maybe even join the SS like you if I'm accepted. I don't want any black marks on my record, sir." Frederick groveled as much as he could without making it to obvious. Frederick admired the Commandant, he was dressed immaculately, and not a hair was out of place. His boots, belt and black gun holster polished to perfection,; they shone like a mirror.

The Commandant was taken by surprise. He sat back and studied the boy. "Do you think I am stupid, boy? Don't patronize me. There's something fishy about this whole thing it stinks. I have nothing to go on, except one small fact. One of the witnesses, namely you, I have seen breaking the law and peddling black market goods. I also know the British aircraft crashed close to your farm, another coincidence. Do you see this?" He chuffed, as he held up a bag containing something heavy and large.

"Yes, sir what is it?"

"It's one of the Colonel's helmets. It was discovered at the burnt hanger. I have an expert arriving in Würzburg tomorrow who will be checking for fingerprints. Apart from the Colonel's, I expect to find those of the people who attacked you and the Colonel at his cottage and stole it. And, of course, the person who wore it. I will of course be looking for a certain elderly gentleman with the same figure. There's of course no reason why this older gentleman's finger prints would be on it unless...?" He paused.

Frederick turned white. He fought with his body to stop it from shaking. The commandant got up and walked over to a large safe. He placed the bag and helmet in the safe and locked it.

"All will be a little clearer tomorrow. You can go for now boy."

Frederick acted dumb. "Em.. I'm not sure what you mean sir, but thank you."

The commandant studied Frederick and eyed him suspiciously. "The coincidences I mentioned is that your name has come across my desk twice in one week. The two Hitler Youth on guard duty at the airport report seeing the Colonel and a member of Hitler Youth and a British airman. We both know it wasn't the Colonel because he was with us when the aircraft took off. They both say the Hitler Youth that was with the Colonel had dark hair, not fair hair, so you're out of the picture again. But I do know you had been trading black market goods with a known member of the Edelweiss Pirates. Did you know this?"

Frederick thought hard about what the waiter had told him. "No sir, the new waiter told me he was a traitor to our country. I never knew he was a Pirate. If I did I would've reported it immediately, sir."

The commandant stood and intensely stared at Frederick. "You may go, but I think we shall be talking again very soon. Do I make myself clear?"

"Yes sir, crystal clear, thank you sir."

The Commandant gestured him out of the office.

Frederick felt sick. He knew Karl's, Fritz's, and his grandfather's prints would be on the helmet. He had to get it before tomorrow. He called an emergency meeting at the barn.

Chapter Thirty-One

"We're sunk," Karl sighed when Frederick broke the news to everyone.

"We have to get that helmet or at least clean off the fingerprints," Grandpa said. "If not, we might as well all leave Würzburg tonight and never return."

They tried coming up with all sorts of ideas from blowing up the safe to stealing the safe. Nothing seemed possible.

"We have to break into the safe. Grandpa; you must know a safe cracker," Eva suggested.

"Why? I'm not a criminal," he shouted. The room went quiet for a few moments before Grandpa spoke again. "I'm sorry for shouting Eva. I am scared for all of our lives."

"We need to open it ourselves. We can break into the offices tonight. Can't we listen at the safe using that thing doctors use to hear your heart?" Eva asked.

"Stethoscope," Karl suggested.

"And were will we get one tonight?" Helmut asked.

"Could we crack it without' a stethoscope?" Frederick asked.

"No," Grandpa explained. "You would need someone who could hear all sorts of high and low frequencies. You need better than normal hearing for that."

The group went quiet again; they seemed doomed.

"Berthold." Karl smiled. They all looked at him like he was crazy.

"Yes, he's blind, but he can hear a pin drop. Literally, he can hear a mouse taking a poo."

The idea of using a blind person to break into a Nazi office and then into a safe seemed like a suicide mission. They thought it was a stupid idea but eventually considered it. They had no other options. Eva left to borrow one of Luis's Hitler Youth uniforms. They met up just after eight that night at Karl's home. When they got there, Berthold and his mother were having an argument. She was totally against the idea. Berthold was determined to help out the Pirates. Eventually she gave in. She hadn't seen him so excited for years. It was if he had suddenly become alive again.

Luis's uniform fitted like a glove. Berthold had a large grin on his face. Eva held his hand while they walked to the Nazi offices. The Nazi offices were once a Jewish owned hotel, but the family was thrown out onto the street and it was taken over.

The walk took just over half an hour. Frederick, Karl, Helmut, and Fritz surrounded Berthold. They all wore their Hitler Youth Uniforms. This way no one would bother them. Holding Eva's hand looked like they were a young couple. Berthold kept his head down. So far it had worked.

"Okay, Berthold, the hotel is just ahead of us. The door is open. A few officers and maybe secretaries will be there. Just hold tight to Eva. Everyone just follow me," Frederick explained.

The door was open just as he had thought. He walked into lobby. A group of six Hitler Youth boys were coming down the stairs. Eva squeezed Berthold's hand tight.

"Where are you going?" the oldest looking one asked. Frederick faced them but was lost for words. Fritz recognized the youth. It was Erwin.

"Well look who it is, the bullies. You bastards kicked the shit out of us when it was ten against four, now it looks even. You want to try it again with Frederick here?" Fritz spat. "Frederick, these are the cowards who kicked the living daylights out of us."

"We never knew you were Hitler Youth. You weren't in uniform." Erwin stood back while Frederick walked closer. They had heard of Frederick from school. They were not about to tangle with him.

"Get out of my sight before I teach you guys a lesson in fighting," Frederick growled. He spat his words in Erwin's face.

"We were just leaving anyway," Erwin croaked.

Frederick led them into the commandant's office. They closed the door behind them. Karl led Berthold over to the safe. He knelt down and felt the dial. Grandpa Gunthrie had explained to him how to do it. He placed his ear on the door and starting turning the dial. The others watched, dreading someone would come in at any moment. For over twenty minutes Berthold turned the dial back and forth. Every now and then he would try the handle. Each time it never worked, so he tried again and again.

"Whoop whoop," cheered Helmut when the door eventually opened with a clunk. Frederick found the helmet in a bag. He put socks on his hands and took it out. Karl passed him a damp cloth. They cleaned it, making sure every fingerprint was gone. They placed it back, locked the safe, and left. On the way home they sang the Edelweiss Pirates song. As they neared Karl and Berthold's home they stopped. Berthold was weeping.

"What's wrong Berthold?" Karl asked, concerned. His weeping continued; he fell down on the ground and sat weeping. Karl's mother was waiting. She had noticed it and rushed out to help.

"What happened? What have you done to him?" she cried. She bent down and helped her son to his feet and gently wiped his tears with her fingers. "Karl, what did you do to him?"

"Nothing. He was happy and singing with us a few minutes ago," Karl said. The others all looked on concerned.

Berthold finally took a breath. "Mother, nothing's wrong with me." He moved forward and kissed her, "For the first time in over ten years, I'm happy. I went on a mission with my little brother and his friends. I held a girl's hand. We sang a funny song walking hand in hand down the lane. I feel alive." Berthold sniffed. "They saved a Jewish girl's life and I helped cover it up. I'm *not* useless. I can do stuff. I'll start playing the piano again. I won't let the Nazis beat me anymore."

Frederick and Fritz both coughed to clear their throats and turned so the others couldn't see as they wiped tears from their eyes. It was considered weak to cry, even for Edelweiss Pirates. Karl and his mother took Berthold inside. He immediately went to the piano.

*

Two days later at school Fritz and Karl both arrived with black eyes. Neither would say what happened. Frederick had taken his revenge for making him strip completely. Frederick was given a bravery medal by the Colonel and was promoted, much to the annoyance of Luis.

"Remarkable young man," the Colonel had told him. "This country could do with a few more young men like you." Luis bit his tongue.

It gave Frederick a much better insight to the workings of the Hitler Youth and a better position to carry out more attacks on the regime. He knew that he had to be much more cautious than before.

He told the other Pirates later the hardest part of the mission was holding himself back when he watched the aircraft soar into the sky. He told them he was so happy he actually had tears in his eyes and it was painful holding back his true feelings, knowing that little Zelda would now be free from the tyranny of the Nazis.

The Edelweiss Pirates continued to grow across Nazi Germany. If they were caught, boys and girls as young as fifteen were shot, imprisoned, or publicly hung. Often, while in prison, they were refused basic human rights that included bedding, clothing, and even food.

Luis was extremely lucky and suffered only minor burns. His throat was sore severely for a few weeks after breathing in hot smoke. Eva told him he should be thankful that Fred saved his life. Luis argued that it was Fred's fault that he became trapped in the first place and Helmut's for breaking the faucet off the fuel tank. Although up to now he had not given them away.

Frederick Weaver flew to Switzerland and managed to land safely. He was taken to the British consultant. After two days he made it back to Britain where he continued to fly Lancaster bombers for the duration of the war. Zelda was given a new home in Switzerland with Grandpa Gunthrie's cousin. She never returned to Germany.

The two Hitler Youth who were on guard duty at the airport were both beaten and sent to the Russian front. They were given a choice of imprisonment or fighting for their county. They both chose the latter. Despite their young age, they were put on the front lines. Neither of the boys returned to Würzburg after the war.

Chapter Thirty-Two

Stroudsburg, PA, 2012

Austin looked wide-eyed at his grandfather. "So did they get shot?"

His grandfather looked sad and pushed his fingers over his balding head. "I try to tell myself sometimes that maybe they met a girl or something and after the bombing of Wurzburg they never returned."

"What bombing Grandpa?" Austin asked. His grandmother came in, followed by his sister.

"Well, Wurzburg was bombed in March of 1945, a month before the war ended. No city sustained more bombs in such a short while. It has never been repeated anywhere."

"Stop telling him war stories, Frederick. The boy will have nightmares," Austin's grandmother protested.

"I need to know. It's for my history project," Austin argued.

"Can I hear them too?" Samantha asked.

"No. Go away. You're too young," Austin snapped.

"Frederick, I need some more milk. Take Austin with you and tell him in the car," Grandma Schmidt told her husband. Samantha was not too pleased with not being able to hear the stories but happy that her grandmother slapped her brother on the top of his head. He ran upstairs, got dressed, and met his grandfather in the garage.

Austin and Frederick climbed into the car and put on their seat belts. "Well what about the bombing?" Austin asked.

"March 16, 1945, Wurzburg was bombed over and over again over. Twelve hundred tons of bombs dropped and over three thousand civilians were killed by the Royal Air Force."

"Do you think Fred bombed your town?"

"I hope not, but if he did he was following orders. The town was destroyed. Almost everyone I knew and loved was killed." As Frederick spoke, his voice started to break. He wiped the tears from his eyes. Austin looked across at his grandfather and chewed his bottom lip.

The car slowly stopped outside the 7/11 store. They sat in silence for a few moments.

"So that was the end of the Edelweiss Pirates?" Austin asked.

His grandfather sighed, cleared his throat, and wiped his eyes. "The squadron leader escaped with little Zelda was in 1942. We had three more years of evading the Nazis, the Colonel, and the

Commandant. But after the March bombings of 1945, there wasn't much left. After the war, everything I knew was destroyed. I moved to my cousin's in Switzerland. But the Pirates had many run-ins with the Nazis. At one point, Fritz was captured." He sighed. "But that's another story."

"What happened to Fritz, Eva Helmut, and Karl?"

"Like I said young man, that's another story."

Austin sat in deep thought. "Your cousin's in Switzerland. That's where you sent Zelda. Did you meet her again?"

His grandfather roared with laughter. His shaky hand gently slapped his grandson's knee. Austin was puzzled by his laughter he smiled and asked again.

"What did I say that's so funny? I thought she was flown to Switzerland to live with your Grandpa Gunthrie's cousin."

"Oh dear boy, you're so funny. Yes, I met Zelda. She was eight years old when I went to Switzerland. She was ten when I left for America. Heartbroken she was."

"You must have been close, like having a little sister. I hate Samantha." He paused for a moment. "Okay I don't hate her, she's just soooooo annoying."

"Austin, we kept in touch when I moved her., I got a job and bought a home. Eight years after moving to America, when I was twenty-seven, my cousin in Switzerland died. Zelda had no real family so she came across to America. She was nineteen and the most beautiful girl I had ever seen. When I met her at the airport she took my breath away."

Austin tried to put the pieces together. "So she lives in America now? Do you still keep in touch?" Austin asked.

"Do you have any brains in there, son?" his grandfather joked, tapping Austin on the side of the head. "In America, Zelda isn't a popular name so she goes by her second name, Hanna. Zelda Hanna Koffler was her full name. Of course, you know her as Hanna Schmidt when she married me, and you call her Grandma."

Austin beamed; the story had a happy ending after all. He wanted to ask his grandfather what happened to Fritz, Helmut, Eva, Karl, and, of course, Grandpa Gunthrie. But he sensed it was still very painful for his grandfather, even after sixty years. One thing was certain; his grandfather did not kill any Jewish people. He had in fact helped them and even married one. Austin was proud to have Jewish ancestry in his blood. He had so much to write about for his history homework. This would wipe the grin off Scott McCamant's face.

*

Easter couldn't come fast enough. Austin was promised a long weekend fishing. Being away from

Samantha and his parents was a bonus enough. Staying up late each night with his grandfather at his fishing lodge was a highlight of the year for Austin, but hearing more stories about what his grandfather did to upset the Nazi war machine was something he would remember for the rest of his life.

More Books by This Author

The Jason Steed Series:

1. Fledgling, Jason Steed

2. Jason Steed, Revenge

3. Jason Steed, Absolutely Nothing

4. Jason Steed, Royal Decree

5. Jason Steed, Face-Off

Archie Wilson & The Nuckelavee

Made in the USA
Lexington, KY
12 October 2018